THE LADIES MAN

uNkosiyazi

ISBN: 978-0-9869764-8-3

DEDICATION

All the women I shared my smile with.

CONTENTS

NU17

11/1/11 3:55:04: UNkosiyazi: i dig yo format- 11:11 11.11.1
11/1/11 3:49:52: NU17: Hey it will be: 11:11 on 11.11.01. Check ur format!
10/16/11 22:34:53: UNkosiyazi: If You Were Here Tonight: Alexander O'Neal
10/16/11 23:53:54: UNkosiyazi: i see you, in a lonely place
10/17/11 0:01:50: UNkosiyazi: there are times, when you'll need someone
10/18/11 2:45:43: UNkosiyazi: on a lighter note: been dreaming about the new "two door" Range Rover.
10/18/11 2:53:29: NU17: Looking fab.
10/18/11 2:54:22: UNkosiyazi: it drives sweet too
10/21/11 18:42:48: UNkosiyazi: <media omitted>
10/21/11 19:17:07: UNkosiyazi: in 2008 in South Africa: 54% Whites graduated with PhD's while Blacks were 13%. what a shame- we need KNOWLEDGE CREATORS. let us pursue high education &encourage others. Whites are going to rule and control us if we are not careful. our children should know from word go that the lowest level of education for them is PhD.
10/22/11 23:49:40: UNkosiyazi: the sun goes away to engage in a serious war against darkness and in the morning it rises to save humankind.
10/23/11 2:00:04: NU17: Humankind is really grateful. Woke up to beautiful sunny morning.
10/23/11 5:08:22: UNkosiyazi: sweet.
10/23/11 5:14:04: NU17: Have u even slept wena?
10/23/11 5:15:44: UNkosiyazi: hahaha...
10/23/11 5:17:38: NU17: hahaha. i c. U're just up very early
10/23/11 5:31:18: UNkosiyazi: gotta go shooting in less than two hours tym.
10/23/11 5:31:34: UNkosiyazi: <media omitted>

10/23/11 5:32:32: NU17: Askis, i didn't know. Hope u feel better soon
10/23/11 5:35:08: UNkosiyazi: thank you.
10/23/11 5:40:37: UNkosiyazi: ...itiz just a change of season and i always change with the season- hahaha...
10/23/11 5:41:55: UNkosiyazi: that clip is from a film im working on.
10/23/11 5:45:40: NU17: Looks interesting
10/23/11 5:50:24: UNkosiyazi: hahaha...
10/23/11 5:50:51: UNkosiyazi: ...not as interesting as you.
10/23/11 5:51:12: NU17: Oh really
10/23/11 5:51:30: UNkosiyazi: yes
10/23/11 5:52:44: NU17: Hahaha.
10/23/11 5:53:51: UNkosiyazi: truth
10/23/11 5:54:10: NU17: i believe u
10/23/11 5:54:39: UNkosiyazi: good
10/23/11 6:00:26: UNkosiyazi: you shuld be a "polygamist" and have two consorts: hahahaha...
10/23/11 6:04:51: NU17: Hahahaha. SA isn't that liberal yet.
10/23/11 6:05:47: UNkosiyazi: interesting: one can always push an envelope.
10/23/11 6:06:26: UNkosiyazi: by da way, the guy that is throwing foliage is Dave Chappelle's step-brother. he is the one who choreographed the fighting scene.
10/23/11 6:08:10: NU17: Be the first female polygamist!
10/23/11 6:11:18: UNkosiyazi: Polyandry
10/23/11 6:15:29: UNkosiyazi: you wont be the first but in recent history u will be. u'll just need to provide a whole lot of concubines for your "lords" to procreate with and spread their surname, not yours.
10/23/11 7:16:44: UNkosiyazi: gotta get ready for work (shoot).
10/24/11 3:03:25: UNkosiyazi: Come Live With Me Angel: Marvin Gaye
10/24/11 14:17:57: UNkosiyazi: <media omitted>
10/24/11 14:18:04: UNkosiyazi: ...this morning around campus.
10/24/11 17:04:44: UNkosiyazi: <media omitted>
10/24/11 17:04:49: UNkosiyazi: ...guess what it is
10/24/11 21:10:29: UNkosiyazi: what is the rate of men marrying virgin women?

10/24/11 21:15:58: UNkosiyazi: a firstborn child born from a virgin woman is special.
10/24/11 21:21:11: UNkosiyazi: a virgin woman (women) in a society / community is PRICELESS.
10/24/11 21:27:50: UNkosiyazi: we need virgins in our society. please encourage girls / ladies you know to preserve their virginity (innocence). it is the "in-thing", it is "sexy".
10/24/11 22:16:59: NU17: Like i did until i was 18. i don't how i'd teach my daughers to do the same
10/24/11 22:19:16: UNkosiyazi: great stuff NU17.
10/24/11 22:22:52: NU17: i will. It's beautiful.
10/24/11 22:29:42: UNkosiyazi: i won't despair.
10/25/11 13:07:04: UNkosiyazi: i wonder if Christianity didn't introduce wedding of the Whites (white wedding) will my sister be so fixated about "walking down the aisle"?
10/25/11 13:08:49: UNkosiyazi: rich and highly educated people of India still have "fixed marriages".
10/25/11 17:50:28: UNkosiyazi: <media omitted>
10/25/11 17:50:34: UNkosiyazi: ...at the end of the day!
10/25/11 17:54:51: UNkosiyazi: <media omitted>
10/25/11 18:04:24: UNkosiyazi: <media omitted>
10/25/11 18:11:26: UNkosiyazi: trick-o-treat night
10/26/11 1:04:24: UNkosiyazi: im tired
10/26/11 1:28:21: NU17: Get some sleep or r u shooting?
10/26/11 1:28:33: NU17: How's the cough?
10/26/11 1:31:35: UNkosiyazi: the cough came and left, that's why im back to my cigar &pipe but havnt been feeling like drinking. im watching what i eat &i take calculated portions.
10/26/11 1:32:01: UNkosiyazi: the shoot was just for the weekend.
10/26/11 1:33:27: UNkosiyazi: ive just got lot on my mind as far as work &projects i have on my plate, so im tired more mentally from mental gymnastics.
10/26/11 1:34:15: UNkosiyazi: ...did i tell you im working on a children's book my kids wrote?
10/26/11 23:31:36: UNkosiyazi: Brown Eyed Girl: Tevin Campbell

10/28/11 0:00:13: UNkosiyazi: time is passing by very fast, i get old everyday and i wonder if i'll ever achieve in time all that i came here on earth for.
10/28/11 2:50:19: NU17: You will, I'm sure u will.
10/28/11 8:43:03: UNkosiyazi: i sure hope too.
10/28/11 9:02:59: NU17: Alibulali
10/28/11 9:21:09: UNkosiyazi: Arab Slave Trade: African-Indians (Siddis), African-Iranians, African-Arabs, African-Pakistanis, the list goes on.
10/28/11 9:22:49: UNkosiyazi: <media omitted>
10/28/11 9:32:47: NU17: Who's this pretty lady?
10/28/11 9:35:33: UNkosiyazi: hahaha...
10/28/11 9:35:59: NU17: "Talking"?
10/28/11 9:36:30: UNkosiyazi: hahaha...
10/28/11 9:37:18: UNkosiyazi: i get to sample all the finest "cuisines" of this world.
10/28/11 9:39:56: NU17: Lmao @ cuisine.
10/28/11 9:41:04: UNkosiyazi: im a lucky man, ancestors have been good to me.
10/28/11 19:52:10: UNkosiyazi: i'll never forget how Sir George Grey used raw trickery on Nongqawuze that almost annihalated the Xhosa people.
10/28/11 20:58:12: UNkosiyazi: Christianity is keeping us contained, pacified and divided.
10/30/11 2:57:11: UNkosiyazi: <media omitted>
10/30/11 3:39:24: UNkosiyazi: Will i live my life chasing after women?
10/30/11 3:43:00: NU17: Damn
10/30/11 3:45:03: NU17: He just put up on fb.
10/31/11 19:16:43: UNkosiyazi: nice song...
10/31/11 20:00:44: UNkosiyazi: To Be Young, Gifted and Black: Donny Hathaway
Nov 01, 2011 is my format.
11/1/11 3:46:04: UNkosiyazi: text me when it's 11:11 11.01.11
11/1/11 2:15:06: UNkosiyazi: gudmornin!
11/1/11 3:18:46: NU17: Hey there
11/1/11 3:20:30: UNkosiyazi: unjani Mntwana?

11/1/11 3:21:55: UNkosiyazi: waz thinkin da ada day, what wuld happen if i got u pregnant?
11/1/11 3:25:16: NU17: Hahaha. Hampa. What got u thinking.
11/1/11 3:37:03: UNkosiyazi: i think a lot.
11/1/11 3:52:15: UNkosiyazi: hahaha...
11/1/11 3:53:47: NU17: Hahaha. American!
11/1/11 3:56:11: UNkosiyazi: say sumthin sweet when u text me around that tym.
11/1/11 3:56:58: NU17: Hahaha. i got something that'll make u smile!
11/1/11 3:58:52: UNkosiyazi: ...im off to sleep.
11/1/11 3:59:39: NU17: Sweet dreams.
11/1/11 12:28:44: UNkosiyazi: ...dont forget to get umsebenzi done for you over the December break.
11/1/11 12:37:53: NU17: Ja. It'll b Jan. Hopefully my mom will agree.
11/1/11 12:40:08: UNkosiyazi: it doesn't matter, umdala anyway and unguMfazi.
11/1/11 12:51:34: NU17: i won't. He's Mormon aswell ngoku, but i know he'll agree
11/1/11 12:58:13: UNkosiyazi: go consult tomorrow when u wake up.
11/1/11 13:32:04: UNkosiyazi: ps: remember that since u r spoken for (married), your husband shuld kno (be consulted / informed).
11/1/11 19:27:41: UNkosiyazi: "Too many drinks have been given to me
11/3/11 9:55:45: UNkosiyazi: <media omitted>
11/4/11 2:21:14: UNkosiyazi: "...this is my moment, i waited all my life. i can tell it's time"
11/4/11 3:27:17: UNkosiyazi: u like: Dance Ass?
11/4/11 3:41:21: UNkosiyazi: "...i think im addicted to naked pictures and sittin talkin bout chicks that we almost had. i dont think im conscious of making monsters outta the women that i sponsor til it all goes bad. but shit it's all gud. we threw a party, yeh we threw a party. chicks came over, yeh we threw a party..."
11/4/11 4:28:34: UNkosiyazi: <media omitted>
11/4/11 4:28:40: UNkosiyazi: im still up in the studio editing my Mozambique film. time is 04:30am
11/4/11 4:35:05: NU17: And when r u going to bed? U need to rest.
11/4/11 4:36:58: UNkosiyazi: cant rest, like a child: im restless.

11/4/11 4:39:20: NU17: And ur energy levels during the day?
11/4/11 4:39:58: UNkosiyazi: coffee
11/4/11 4:40:28: NU17: Addict!
11/4/11 4:42:20: UNkosiyazi: not really, only when need arise.
11/4/11 4:43:57: NU17: Oh good.
11/4/11 4:55:42: UNkosiyazi: it's just like sex.
11/4/11 4:57:06: UNkosiyazi: tell me, where are the Mahlangabeza guys?
11/4/11 5:05:09: NU17: Bakhona
11/4/11 5:05:26: UNkosiyazi: up to what?
11/4/11 5:18:25: UNkosiyazi: im up chasing my dreams, they pass me by when im sleeping.
11/4/11 5:43:46: UNkosiyazi: ...jus got home.
11/4/11 5:55:26: UNkosiyazi: it must be the coffee i drank midnight but im feelin horny, got a pounding erection.
11/4/11 6:11:55: NU17: It's the coffee.
11/4/11 6:15:24: UNkosiyazi: culd it be just nature calling?
11/4/11 6:16:17: NU17: U need to respond then
11/4/11 6:20:07: UNkosiyazi: ...but u r not here.
11/5/11 12:55:00: UNkosiyazi: unjani?
11/5/11 13:08:53: NU17: Ndigood unjani wena?
11/5/11 13:12:33: UNkosiyazi: ndiright nami, jus relaxin &readin.
11/5/11 13:13:16: NU17: What u reading?
11/5/11 13:13:49: UNkosiyazi: business law
11/5/11 13:21:24: UNkosiyazi: i miss my granny, just thinkin bout her.
11/5/11 18:29:25: UNkosiyazi: craving oven-roasted butternut, chicken, sweetpotato, carrots and potatoes.
11/5/11 20:46:27: UNkosiyazi: ps: next time when we get together remember to take full advantage of the opportunity.
11/8/11 11:09:35: NU17: UNkosiyazi UNkosiyazi. Unjani? Unqabile. Ndiyakukhumbula.
11/8/11 12:20:58: UNkosiyazi: uyazi ngihlala ngikucabanga... dont ever wonder.
11/8/11 12:21:15: UNkosiyazi: unjani wena Sthandwa sami?
11/8/11 12:23:02: NU17: Good to hear from. @least i know why u've been scarce. I'm doing good thanks.

11/8/11 12:32:38: UNkosiyazi: bakuphethe kahle emsebenzini?
11/8/11 12:32:46: UNkosiyazi: ?
11/8/11 12:33:49: NU17: Bantwana bandiphethe GR8, work is going well and husband is ok
11/8/11 12:35:23: UNkosiyazi: "ok"?
11/8/11 12:43:02: NU17: Communication is ZERO. He's just given up on our marriage. Hates my going out, drinking, socializing. He'd prefer me being @ home like i used and i can't.
11/8/11 12:54:39: UNkosiyazi: ngiyakuzwa.
11/8/11 13:13:27: NU17: Hope fully. It's been 2 years
11/8/11 13:56:31: UNkosiyazi: it's none of my bizness, but what r both your parents saying?
11/8/11 14:07:03: NU17: Haven't spoken to them
11/8/11 14:08:35: UNkosiyazi: what are you waiting for?
11/8/11 14:10:31: NU17: Where do i even start. i want to stay but things are hard right now.
11/8/11 14:16:45: UNkosiyazi: act!
11/8/11 14:18:24: NU17: Fear of the unknown
11/8/11 14:38:17: UNkosiyazi: you're an Aquarian: take your chances.
11/8/11 14:41:19: NU17: Lindo.
11/8/11 14:45:08: UNkosiyazi: NU17.
11/8/11 14:46:16: NU17: Hahaha. Andayihleka
11/8/11 15:19:24: UNkosiyazi: hah!
11/8/11 15:24:58: UNkosiyazi: on a lighter note, do you know the reality show called: LOVE &HIPHOP?
11/8/11 15:28:33: NU17: Nope
11/8/11 16:22:06: UNkosiyazi: some "weird" show about these five women: Mashonda (Swiss Beatz ex-wife), Chrissy (Jim Jones fiancee), Olivia (ex-G-Unit member), Somaya (aspiring artist who is friends with rest of women), Emily (Fabulous baby-mama / girlfrind) i dont even know what do show is about, ive just consumed 6 episodes and still confused about what it's about. i guess u can say it's about hiphop industry.
11/11/11 11:11:42: UNkosiyazi: 11:11 11.11.11
11/11/11 1:12:10: UNkosiyazi: 1:11 11.11.11
11/11/11 1:23:44: NU17: Eweeeeeeeee
11/11/11 4:11:40: NU17: It's now officially. 11:11 on 11:11:11

11/11/11 11:16:28: NU17: Mwah
11/16/11 2:01:52: UNkosiyazi: my upcoming Portuguese film...
11/17/11 16:12:36: UNkosiyazi: im thinkin bout SA.
11/17/11 17:45:12: UNkosiyazi: <media omitted>
11/18/11 21:13:54: UNkosiyazi: <media omitted>
11/18/11 21:14:01: UNkosiyazi: missing amawings...
11/18/11 21:54:50: UNkosiyazi: <media omitted>
11/18/11 21:55:01: UNkosiyazi: my food (rooibos tea, wings, rice, potatoes w/Mayo) is ready.
11/19/11 1:52:36: NU17: Ndicela iwings.
11/19/11 10:53:10: UNkosiyazi: hahaha...
11/20/11 3:28:28: UNkosiyazi: "Girls, I ask em do they smoke?
11/20/11 20:17:22: UNkosiyazi: <media omitted>
11/21/11 1:17:16: UNkosiyazi: Same Ole Love: Anita Baker
11/23/11 6:53:42: UNkosiyazi: Girls, I ask em do they smoke?
11/23/11 7:48:54: UNkosiyazi: is there a way you can get me the track titled JIKWA IMALI by Magesh (Tokollo)?
11/23/11 7:52:21: NU17: i can try for u
11/23/11 23:22:19: UNkosiyazi: <media omitted>
11/23/11 23:22:30: UNkosiyazi: Thanksgiving
11/24/11 2:17:27: NU17: Good day sir
11/24/11 7:31:41: UNkosiyazi: a good day (morning) it is indeed.
11/24/11 8:41:35: NU17: It's good. It's raining cats and dogs.
11/24/11 8:49:18: UNkosiyazi: interestin...
11/24/11 8:52:45: NU17: BMW in el today
11/24/11 8:54:57: UNkosiyazi: what does that mean?
11/24/11 8:56:47: NU17: Baby making weather
11/24/11 8:58:27: UNkosiyazi: hahaha...
11/24/11 13:25:10: NU17: Happy Thanksgiving
11/24/11 15:59:54: UNkosiyazi: hahaha...
11/24/11 21:19:29: UNkosiyazi: bottle after bottle till i get messed up.
11/24/11 21:57:50: UNkosiyazi: tell me, what's that song about Tkzee "ela ngwana wa ka..."?
11/26/11 1:24:38: UNkosiyazi: good morning!
11/26/11 1:24:56: NU17: Heya. Howzit goin
11/26/11 1:25:46: UNkosiyazi: just chillin with them dudes...

```
11/26/11 1:27:55: NU17: I'm @ work **crying face**
11/26/11 1:28:59: UNkosiyazi: u do Saturdays too?
11/26/11 1:29:25: NU17: 2 saturdays a month.
11/26/11 1:31:34: UNkosiyazi: full day?
11/26/11 1:36:28: NU17: Until 1
11/26/11 1:39:02: UNkosiyazi: is that considered half-day?
11/26/11 1:39:26: NU17: Yep.
11/26/11 1:40:47: UNkosiyazi: oh well, bear your cross.
11/26/11 1:46:08: NU17: Cz i andina choice.
11/26/11 1:49:32: UNkosiyazi: one day it will make sense.
11/26/11 3:00:31: UNkosiyazi: love without limit
11/26/11 10:17:27: UNkosiyazi: i suppose your day went well.
11/27/11 1:38:37: UNkosiyazi: how did you sleep?
11/27/11 4:23:14: NU17: Hey lindo
11/27/11 4:23:21: NU17: Had our year function izolo
11/27/11 4:23:27: NU17: Just woke up
11/27/11 7:51:40: UNkosiyazi: hahaha...
11/27/11 7:54:38: NU17: Yeah.  Too much
11/27/11 8:03:01: UNkosiyazi: good for you.
11/28/11 0:23:03: UNkosiyazi: goodmorning!
11/29/11 0:41:58: UNkosiyazi: hope you slept well.
11/29/11 1:02:38: NU17: i did thank u.  How's ur day?
11/29/11 1:04:00: UNkosiyazi: im listenin to House while sippin
Southern Comfort.
11/29/11 1:04:05: UNkosiyazi: "i just cant believe that you've been
sent to me from above. you're my angel of love. i cant wait to feel
your sunshine..."
11/29/11 1:06:17: NU17: My favourite...i can even taste it! With just
ice.
11/29/11 1:07:50: UNkosiyazi: i'll drink one for you on your behalf.
11/29/11 1:08:06: NU17: Ndiyabulela
11/29/11 1:08:33: UNkosiyazi: wamukelekile
11/29/11 1:09:01: NU17: Lol.  Having yoghurt and cereal.
11/29/11 1:17:00: UNkosiyazi: mmmhhhmmm...
11/29/11 1:17:14: UNkosiyazi: <media omitted>
11/29/11 2:24:11: NU17: Mmmmmmmmhhhhhhmmm.
```

11/29/11 14:44:26: UNkosiyazi:
http://www.realtor.com/blogs/2011/11/23/bruce-willis-lists-idaho-
home-photos/
11/29/11 15:26:53: NU17: <media omitted>
11/29/11 15:27:54: UNkosiyazi: Yummy
11/29/11 15:28:55: NU17: Hampa.
11/29/11 15:29:32: NU17: Sethu in the middle and yonela on the right
11/29/11 15:29:37: NU17: <media omitted>
11/29/11 15:32:11: UNkosiyazi: you guys look immaculate and full of
youth. i like it.
11/29/11 15:33:56: NU17: Yep u do. We were all young women @ the
same time
11/29/11 15:34:59: NU17: Me @ work
11/29/11 15:35:16: NU17: <media omitted>
11/29/11 15:36:24: NU17: Mommy dearest
11/29/11 15:36:24: NU17: <media omitted>
11/29/11 15:36:52: UNkosiyazi: back then you were "young girls" now
you are Young Women.
11/29/11 15:37:14: UNkosiyazi: nice... your mother still in Europe?
11/29/11 15:37:19: NU17: Yeah. Thought i should update u.
11/29/11 15:37:31: NU17: <media omitted>
11/29/11 15:37:44: NU17: Yep. She's coming down end of Dec for New
Years
11/29/11 15:38:20: UNkosiyazi: im lovin it...
11/29/11 15:39:46: NU17: 2nd trip to cape town with colleagues
11/29/11 15:39:52: NU17: <media omitted>
11/29/11 15:42:41: NU17: <media omitted>
11/29/11 15:43:31: UNkosiyazi: she looks familiar, who is she?
11/29/11 15:44:02: NU17: Lady from kwaMashu. Met her @ training
11/29/11 15:45:14: UNkosiyazi: oh.
11/29/11 15:45:38: NU17: i'll send u 1 last 1.
11/29/11 15:46:53: NU17: <media omitted>
11/29/11 15:47:29: UNkosiyazi: why 1 last 1? im still waitin 4 a "g-
string" one.
11/29/11 15:48:41: NU17: Laughing my freakin ass
off!!!!!!!!!!!!!!!!!!!!!!!!!!!!!!!!!!! Don't have any of those
11/29/11 15:49:55: NU17: <media omitted>

11/29/11 15:50:52: UNkosiyazi: hahaha...
11/29/11 15:51:45: NU17: Haahhaha. Meant pics in those.
11/29/11 15:53:26: UNkosiyazi: ol im sayin: im still waitin...
11/29/11 15:54:13: NU17: Lindoo.
11/29/11 15:54:37: UNkosiyazi: NU17 aka Yummy
11/29/11 15:56:49: NU17: U'll c it when when we start making babies
11/29/11 15:58:20: UNkosiyazi: if that's the case, then PATIENCE IS VIRTUE!
11/29/11 16:00:51: NU17: Hell yes
11/29/11 16:03:19: UNkosiyazi: we've got 11 years anyway, waiting a lil longer will not hurt / deter.
11/29/11 16:40:40: UNkosiyazi: <media omitted>
11/29/11 16:40:42: UNkosiyazi: detoxing...
11/30/11 16:06:02: UNkosiyazi: Classic material indeed... http://yourblackwoman.blogspot.com/2011/12/meet-sara-bartman-original-video-vixen.html#more
12/1/11 15:15:06: UNkosiyazi: A spiritually evolved woman understands the difference between chasing men and choosing a husband. The difference has a profound effect on the quality of life for her, her offspring and her community. Strong married couples build wealthy families which, in turn, build affluent communities. When the majority of babies are born to single individuals, or into marriages that don‚Äôt last, you can‚Äôt sustain an economically sound community. There is a lack of physical comfort because we are not pooling resources. People are fighting over child support and stretching one income among several households.
12/2/11 1:26:42: UNkosiyazi: how did you sleep?
12/2/11 1:34:23: NU17: Hayfever and sinus. But i slept well.
12/2/11 1:36:34: UNkosiyazi: is it seasonal?
12/2/11 1:37:01: NU17: Yep. Affects my daughter aswell.
12/2/11 1:39:19: UNkosiyazi: not good.
12/2/11 1:39:43: NU17: Really not good.
12/2/11 1:40:11: UNkosiyazi: any traditional Xhosa ways of curing / preventing it?
12/2/11 1:42:06: NU17: Don't know.
12/2/11 1:44:26: NU17: i've never had a look.

12/2/11 1:47:22: UNkosiyazi: there is a show here in America on NatGeo where they take sick and afflicted people to the so-called "primitive" people for them to cure them using traditional (they call it "alternative medicine").
12/2/11 15:11:35: UNkosiyazi: <media omitted>
12/2/11 15:46:49: UNkosiyazi: <media omitted>
12/3/11 0:04:33: UNkosiyazi: mornin! is it a gud one or what?
12/3/11 15:35:09: UNkosiyazi: Lay down here beside me and we‚Äôll cruise the caravan
12/4/11 12:56:07: UNkosiyazi: <media omitted>
12/4/11 12:56:12: UNkosiyazi: howaz yo day?
12/4/11 13:09:08: UNkosiyazi: <media omitted>
12/4/11 15:59:50: UNkosiyazi: sweet dreams.
12/4/11 16:00:42: NU17: Izolo couldn't even type. Had hennesy dashed nge amarula.
12/4/11 16:00:54: NU17: Today biyiSouthern Comfort
12/4/11 16:02:47: UNkosiyazi: awuthethi inyani...
12/4/11 16:05:29: NU17: Just crawled into bed. Epic weekend
12/4/11 16:25:45: UNkosiyazi: i envy you.
12/4/11 18:25:59: UNkosiyazi: Sthandwa sami, can u do me a favor? my snuff supply is almost depleted, will you mail (post) me some? nid two or three containers.
12/5/11 12:13:47: UNkosiyazi: Sthandwa sami, can u do me a favor? my snuff supply is almost depleted, will you mail (post) me some? nid two or three containers.
12/5/11 12:14:38: NU17: Stuff like?
12/5/11 12:14:52: UNkosiyazi: snuff
12/5/11 12:15:38: NU17: Oh not stuff, snuff.
12/5/11 12:15:39: NU17: As in the stuff in the blue and yellow container?
12/5/11 12:15:39: NU17: Bendilele askis
12/5/11 12:16:45: UNkosiyazi: exactly
12/5/11 12:18:59: NU17: Ndibroke ngoku, i can do it after the 15th. Akukho too late?
12/5/11 12:20:01: UNkosiyazi: okay, i can wait.
12/5/11 12:20:11: UNkosiyazi: thanks a lot

12/5/11 12:21:37: NU17: No problem. Remind me again around the 13th please
12/5/11 12:22:44: UNkosiyazi: will do
12/5/11 12:23:10: NU17: Usenzani isnuff?
12/5/11 12:27:21: UNkosiyazi: i use it to talk to my grandmothers when i leave the house or wherever i am. it's like a rosary or thusby that reminds me to pray (talk) to my caregivers (ancestors).
12/5/11 12:28:16: NU17: Hahaha @ deep doctrine. It is.
12/5/11 12:31:23: UNkosiyazi: hahaha...
12/5/11 12:32:48: NU17: Lesson learnt
12/5/11 12:34:35: UNkosiyazi: for you baby, it's for free. im starting to charge others for this kind of valuable information.
12/5/11 12:36:54: NU17: U r far too kind. Ndiyabulela mna.
12/5/11 12:38:48: UNkosiyazi: anytime.
12/5/11 12:40:15: NU17: How's ur day?
12/5/11 12:45:44: UNkosiyazi: jus barely got up, stayed up till late last night- eating and drinkin...
12/5/11 12:47:26: NU17: Sounds like the weekend i had
12/5/11 12:51:04: UNkosiyazi: oh stop it, your weekends makes my weekends look like a prayer service.
12/5/11 12:55:46: NU17: Hai Lindo. Prayer service. Hahahahahaha.
12/5/11 12:59:08: UNkosiyazi: Ewe! you party hard. i have to take pointers from you.
12/5/11 13:05:13: NU17: Think it's my friends kanti not me.
12/5/11 13:07:31: UNkosiyazi: allow me to say: you party so well just like your friends.
12/5/11 13:09:26: NU17: Hahaha! Andiyihleka.
12/5/11 13:09:31: NU17: i'll accept that
12/5/11 13:19:21: UNkosiyazi: please do because it is my honest observation.
12/5/11 13:22:50: NU17: Hopefully my festive season will continue like this.
12/5/11 13:26:48: UNkosiyazi: whatever it is that you do: ENJOY!
12/5/11 13:29:36: NU17: My moms coming back nge28th, i have to be a Mormon girl/wife/mother.
12/5/11 13:30:27: UNkosiyazi: ...that shouldn't be hard to do.

12/5/11 13:31:15: UNkosiyazi: just stay balanced: take the good with the bad.
12/5/11 13:32:06: NU17: She still thinks I'm 17
12/5/11 14:41:09: UNkosiyazi: hahaha... mommy's girl!
12/5/11 14:44:32: NU17: I'm not. Qha yena she's living in the past
12/5/11 15:13:11: UNkosiyazi: she will always "live in the past", you'll probably do the same with your offspring too.
12/6/11 23:23:28: UNkosiyazi: i like this Luther song:
12/7/11 11:18:51: UNkosiyazi: seems like it is going to be a good show for the Emerging Black Middle Class on SABC1:
12/7/11 20:21:21: UNkosiyazi: <media omitted>
12/7/11 20:29:41: UNkosiyazi: i did a film about President Zuma before he came into power, and i have never showed it to anyone. im wondering if time is right for me to release it now or should i wait until end of next year?
12/7/11 23:23:25: NU17: They r voting again next year in Mangaung and he could lose his sit as ANC president. There's a big power struggle leading to Mangaung 2012
12/7/11 23:28:57: UNkosiyazi: when next year?
12/7/11 23:57:34: UNkosiyazi: <media omitted>
12/7/11 23:57:42: UNkosiyazi: a teaser... hah!
12/8/11 0:14:02: UNkosiyazi: <media omitted>
12/8/11 0:24:40: UNkosiyazi: <media omitted>
12/8/11 1:56:55: UNkosiyazi: ps: the Children's Book is ready, for now it is just art (drawings) with date stamps and titles.
12/8/11 2:16:55: NU17: i'll have a look for it.
12/8/11 2:18:48: UNkosiyazi: please
12/8/11 2:25:20: UNkosiyazi: some dreams stay dreams and others dreams come true.
12/8/11 2:28:43: UNkosiyazi: Liquid Deep says: "...never let go of your dreams. no matter how hard it may seem."
12/8/11 2:28:53: NU17: This is a perfect 1 to come true. Kids will love it
12/8/11 2:29:09: NU17: Each and every single 1.
12/8/11 2:32:09: UNkosiyazi: in uNkulunkulu we trust!!!
12/10/11 0:46:38: UNkosiyazi: <media omitted>
12/10/11 0:46:39: UNkosiyazi: gudmornin!

12/10/11 0:47:56: NU17: Hey there
12/10/11 2:33:11: UNkosiyazi: hey hey...
12/10/11 2:50:31: NU17: Hw r u doing?
12/10/11 2:51:40: UNkosiyazi: <media omitted>
12/10/11 2:51:49: UNkosiyazi: Smoking
12/10/11 12:52:07: UNkosiyazi: AmaPantsula Ajabulile = Professor ft
Kabelo
12/10/11 12:52:56: NU17: Love that song!
12/10/11 12:53:32: NU17: Have u listened to the new BIG NUZ album
12/10/11 12:54:01: UNkosiyazi: not yet, is it dope?
12/10/11 12:57:16: UNkosiyazi: only know Ungazoba Serious = Big NUZ.
12/10/11 13:01:24: NU17: Too dope.
12/10/11 13:03:13: UNkosiyazi: yep!
12/10/11 13:07:24: NU17: It is. Plus it's double cd.
12/10/11 13:08:26: UNkosiyazi: sweet
12/10/11 13:24:02: NU17: <media omitted>
12/10/11 13:24:36: NU17: That's my favourite in the album
12/10/11 13:31:44: UNkosiyazi: love it... about my fav subject.
12/10/11 13:34:15: NU17: Loved the first time i heart it
12/10/11 13:37:00: UNkosiyazi: cant stop listenin to it, thanks.
12/10/11 13:37:40: NU17: Only a pleasure
12/11/11 13:19:37: UNkosiyazi: <media omitted>
12/11/11 14:58:27: UNkosiyazi: ulale kahle
12/11/11 17:14:09: UNkosiyazi: <media omitted>
12/12/11 1:10:12: UNkosiyazi: how did you sleep?
12/12/11 1:11:41: NU17: Very well thank you
12/12/11 9:25:52: UNkosiyazi: that is gud to know, ive jus got up to.
thankful for another new day to learn or do something new.
12/12/11 9:26:18: NU17: Good morning
12/12/11 9:28:19: UNkosiyazi: oh thank u...
12/12/11 9:28:56: NU17: Oh no. U need company.
12/12/11 9:29:47: UNkosiyazi: yep!
12/12/11 10:06:35: UNkosiyazi: time's a wastin!
12/12/11 10:12:19: UNkosiyazi: it inspires me this Erykah Badu song:
12/12/11 10:53:58: UNkosiyazi: in my dream last night, a woman was
teaching me some deep doctrine and showing me some signs: i dont

really recollect it all but i believe it was a sign of things to come that i will learn.
12/12/11 13:54:30: UNkosiyazi: Meet Sara Bartman: The Original Video Vixen
12/13/11 15:11:31: UNkosiyazi: before you lay yourself down to sleep tonight, know that im glad i know you and wish you well in all your dreams.
12/13/11 15:14:35: NU17: Oh wow thank you.
12/13/11 15:14:37: NU17: Continue to have a good day.
12/13/11 15:17:48: UNkosiyazi: ...will do, thanks a lot!
12/13/11 15:18:22: NU17: Ndispeechless.
12/13/11 15:19:38: UNkosiyazi: hah!
12/13/11 15:20:37: NU17: Lesson learnt
12/13/11 15:21:37: UNkosiyazi: you also play a part in my existence.
12/13/11 15:26:13: NU17: How?
12/13/11 15:33:42: UNkosiyazi: we've known each other so long and we've always been cool. you listen when i talk and you talk to me also. it's not by chance we're still talkin. there is a role you play in my existence (life). you dont have to be my wife to be special to me.
12/13/11 15:34:59: NU17: Hahaha @ the last sentence. But uthetha inyani.
12/13/11 21:52:10: UNkosiyazi: Amber Riley reminds me of you.
12/14/11 0:03:29: UNkosiyazi: <media omitted>
12/14/11 3:26:27: UNkosiyazi: five Corona's, im feeling nice.
12/14/11 3:27:21: NU17: Beer or cider
12/14/11 3:27:48: UNkosiyazi: Beer
12/14/11 3:49:09: UNkosiyazi: im excited coz i re-started (resumed) my Zulu novel today.
12/14/11 3:59:31: NU17: Before my girls went on holiday, i started reading xhosa books to them.
12/14/11 4:00:15: NU17: I'm enjoying it alot
12/14/11 4:00:19: UNkosiyazi: good stuff, keep it up.
12/14/11 4:00:46: UNkosiyazi: ...guess what my Zulu novel is about?
12/14/11 4:09:13: UNkosiyazi: <media omitted>
12/14/11 4:09:14: UNkosiyazi: im attacking Heineken now, cant stop,
12/14/11 4:15:10: UNkosiyazi: <media omitted>

12/14/11 5:00:20: NU17: What's the novel about
12/14/11 5:01:06: UNkosiyazi: i said guess.
12/14/11 5:01:21: NU17: Haike lindo ke
12/14/11 5:02:15: UNkosiyazi: okay, since u dont wanna guess, im off
to sleep. it's five in the morning anyway.
12/14/11 5:04:32: NU17: About love
12/14/11 5:05:37: UNkosiyazi: hahaha... love and?
12/14/11 5:10:27: NU17: Money
12/14/11 5:11:04: UNkosiyazi: hahaha... no!
12/14/11 5:17:14: NU17: Hahaha. Love and war?
12/14/11 5:19:01: UNkosiyazi: hahaha... nope!
12/14/11 5:23:47: NU17: Lala kakhle ke cz i've run out guesses
12/14/11 11:14:15: UNkosiyazi: hahaha...
12/14/11 11:18:25: NU17: Hahaha. How would i have guessed that?
12/14/11 11:20:03: UNkosiyazi: that's why im making you guess.
12/14/11 11:20:35: NU17: Am still supposed to guessing *hiding*
12/14/11 11:22:15: UNkosiyazi: yeah, i've given you a hint also.
you've mentioned "love" already, what else?
12/14/11 11:24:32: NU17: What domestification in Zulu?
12/14/11 11:27:41: UNkosiyazi: hahaha! what is it in isiXhosa?
12/14/11 11:28:11: NU17: Andiyazi
12/14/11 11:29:17: UNkosiyazi: hah!
12/14/11 11:29:56: NU17: It's ukukhuthala, i thing
12/14/11 11:30:25: UNkosiyazi: you're funny: hahaha...
12/14/11 11:30:45: NU17: hahaha
12/14/11 11:34:39: UNkosiyazi: lemme just say: watch the space.
12/14/11 11:35:22: NU17: i know tell me sometime soon
12/14/11 11:37:06: UNkosiyazi: i was so disappointed a little last
year when i finished my Braamfontein novel and could not publish it
because it became "potent" and i decided to shelve it and to write
another one.
12/14/11 11:38:21: UNkosiyazi: these things are easy, just write one
too.
12/14/11 13:53:25: NU17: i need to start keeping a journal again
12/14/11 14:14:46: UNkosiyazi: ...dont keep it the way Mormons do,
keep it for your future generations that will see through you what

used to happen in your days. dont drown it in that church jargon and feelings.
12/14/11 14:17:48: NU17: That's why i stopped keeping 1.
12/14/11 14:19:51: UNkosiyazi: that's why i stopped writing mine too. my thoughts and feelings i write them as short stories or poetry or prose.
12/14/11 14:21:29: NU17: i'll c if i can start 1 ngelohlobo
12/14/11 14:22:54: UNkosiyazi: i learnt: the game (stories) is to sold not told.
12/14/11 14:23:13: UNkosiyazi: "be"
12/14/11 14:24:33: UNkosiyazi: it's like the stealing or prostituting our mineral resources.
12/14/11 14:48:02: UNkosiyazi: <media omitted>
12/14/11 23:09:34: UNkosiyazi: gudmornin!
12/14/11 23:13:50: UNkosiyazi: you can mail me two or three snuffs. they are about 4 / 5 bucks each. you can put them on a small yellow padded envelope and mail them on a regular rate and dont insure them.
12/14/11 23:14:20: UNkosiyazi: ps: are you banking with FNB?
12/14/11 23:21:52: NU17: Yes i am
12/14/11 23:31:21: UNkosiyazi: ...just get me a quote and i'll reimburse you.
12/14/11 23:32:14: NU17: Will do.
12/14/11 23:32:34: UNkosiyazi: thanks
12/17/11 22:05:22: UNkosiyazi: <media omitted>
12/19/11 1:20:41: UNkosiyazi: ...dont tell me you are still sleepin! rise and shine, it's a new day. enjoy it.
12/19/11 1:44:00: NU17: I'm @ work.
12/19/11 1:44:07: NU17: i wish i was sleeping
12/19/11 1:44:53: UNkosiyazi: hahaha...
12/19/11 1:45:06: UNkosiyazi: enjoy your day!
12/19/11 1:46:46: NU17: This is too sad.
12/19/11 1:47:12: UNkosiyazi: very sad...
12/19/11 1:47:27: UNkosiyazi: ...and very bad.
12/19/11 1:47:31: UNkosiyazi: ive concluded that for me, im just gonna find someone who just wanna put family before career. there turn to be unnecessary competition when both r pushing career coz

family (children) get compromised under the guise of "children are
expensive".
12/19/11 2:28:09: UNkosiyazi: ps: the CNN guy is crying over the fact
that Kobe Bryant's wife is gonna part with half of Kobe's millions,
joint custody of the children and alimony.
12/19/11 2:31:39: UNkosiyazi: traditional marriage is the way to
protect the interests of the children.
12/19/11 2:48:17: UNkosiyazi: what does she want to do with my
property? my brothers are the ones to look after my property when im
gone, not umfazi. they look after my property and children until my
male children are grown ukuvusa umuzi wami (uyise wabo).
12/19/11 23:11:11: UNkosiyazi: i feel creative juices tonight so
lemme share a piece i've just thought about:
12/20/11 13:23:03: UNkosiyazi: <media omitted>
12/20/11 13:34:46: NU17: How often do u smoke?
12/20/11 14:01:21: UNkosiyazi: when a need arise. once every other
three or five days. it depends on the mood im in.
12/20/11 14:42:43: UNkosiyazi: before i forget and get caught up,
lemme say: enjoy your festive season (in Zulu it's called Ishwama /
feast of the first fruits or harvest)!
12/21/11 4:02:13: UNkosiyazi: <media omitted>
12/21/11 4:28:06: NU17: Hahaha
12/21/11 20:10:01: UNkosiyazi: <media omitted>
12/21/11 23:38:35: UNkosiyazi: hey, Kholeka says: Hi!
12/21/11 23:39:17: UNkosiyazi: ...she vaguely remembers going EL and
playing with your brothers.
12/21/11 23:42:11: NU17: Ncooooooh.
12/21/11 23:42:20: NU17: Hiiiiiii!
12/21/11 23:45:54: UNkosiyazi: <media omitted>
12/22/11 0:09:44: UNkosiyazi: i love sleeping on the floor...
12/23/11 1:18:19: UNkosiyazi: here is the link to children art book
by my kids:
http://www.amazon.com/gp/aw/d/B006P16D1I/ref=redir_mdp_mobile
12/23/11 1:56:27: UNkosiyazi: the book is titled: CHICKENS AND GOATS
12/23/11 2:04:28: UNkosiyazi: please support it, rate it and jot a
review while at it... much appreciated.

12/23/11 2:59:35: UNkosiyazi: AS I LAY ME DOWN TO SLEEP, WORDS FROM YASIIN BEY (AN ARTIST FORMERLY KNOWN AS MOS DEF) RINGS IN MY EARS WHEN HE SAYS:
12/23/11 9:25:27: UNkosiyazi: i had a gud sleep... woke up thinking:
12/23/11 10:17:58: UNkosiyazi: <media omitted>
12/23/11 10:18:01: UNkosiyazi: make time to read this. his company owns LVMH (Louis Vutton, Hennessy, Moet), Cartier, Alfred Dunhill, etc...
12/23/11 10:29:28: NU17: Oh my word. It's going into my january budget!
12/23/11 11:53:05: UNkosiyazi: hahaha...
12/24/11 0:22:04: UNkosiyazi: you studying anything next year or you finishing something you started?
12/24/11 0:22:13: UNkosiyazi: ps: good morning! how did you sleep?
12/24/11 0:35:09: NU17: Well hey
12/24/11 0:35:15: NU17: Thanks, hw r u?
12/24/11 0:42:54: UNkosiyazi: im lovely, just planning what to do next?
12/24/11 0:42:59: UNkosiyazi: you studying anything next year or you finishing something you started?
12/24/11 1:01:04: NU17: Starting something new. A+ (IT)
12/24/11 1:01:33: NU17: Caught my husband with a girl @ hemingways mall tonights ago
12/24/11 1:04:49: UNkosiyazi: okay, what is your goal in life, personally?
12/24/11 1:08:51: UNkosiyazi: <media omitted>
12/24/11 1:10:05: NU17: i was IT specialist @ Vodacom and wanted to study that further. i really loved it.
12/24/11 1:14:33: UNkosiyazi: so you are fine with being employed and not employing?
12/24/11 1:17:35: NU17: Have study IT further to be the employer. i was never happy being employed.
12/24/11 1:21:31: UNkosiyazi: good.
12/24/11 1:22:36: UNkosiyazi: okay, back to your "mall" matter. do you have fotoz of your "future" equal?
12/24/11 1:25:46: NU17: No i have a witness. Was with a friend. He admitted to it aswell. Then denied it yesterday

12/24/11 1:29:17: UNkosiyazi: why did you make him admit?
12/24/11 1:29:37: UNkosiyazi: what were you aiming to achieve?
12/24/11 1:31:40: NU17: i didn't. i asked him what i saw and how had it been going on.
12/24/11 1:31:54: NU17: He said it had been going on for 2 weeks
12/24/11 1:38:14: UNkosiyazi: ...dont compete with him.
12/24/11 1:38:41: NU17: How am i competing with him?
12/24/11 1:39:46: UNkosiyazi: you using words like "cheating". men dont cheat.
12/24/11 1:41:01: NU17: Oh. What do they do.
12/24/11 1:41:36: UNkosiyazi: they are polygamous.
12/24/11 1:43:10: NU17: i didn't agree to it then. He lied about his whereabouts. i just happened to b in the area to c it
12/24/11 1:43:31: UNkosiyazi: im sure you were confrontational on your approach when you asked him about it.
12/24/11 1:44:46: NU17: i wasn't.
12/24/11 1:45:36: UNkosiyazi: ...you didnt or dont have to agree to it, it is something you should have been taught when you were young or before you got married or now that you are grown.
12/24/11 1:46:23: UNkosiyazi: ...dont compete with him. like i said before, just because you prefer to give him two beautiful girls, it doesnt mean that that is what he wants. help (support) him to raise his father's house.
12/24/11 1:46:53: NU17: Yho haike. Asoze.
12/24/11 1:48:10: NU17: So i must accept him other women in his life in the day and age of HIV/Aids and STI's
12/24/11 1:49:19: UNkosiyazi: atleast you'll get to keep your husband otherwise that lady is going to take him.
12/24/11 1:50:46: UNkosiyazi: im sincere with you NU17, accept the fact that there are other women out there who would love to carry his seed.
12/24/11 1:56:59: NU17: They have him then. Cz i will sit @ home and wait for HIV to come knocking.
12/24/11 2:00:04: UNkosiyazi: what is this obsession with HIV? cant it be "sit @ home and wait for CHILDREN to come knocking" for you to kiss them.

12/24/11 2:02:42: UNkosiyazi: it's your man's children, you are the senior wife. if you are worried about diseases, help him choose better.
12/24/11 2:05:21: NU17: He did
12/24/11 2:06:56: NU17: i didn't sign up for that. No thanks.
12/24/11 2:09:03: UNkosiyazi: marriage is not a contract as the Whites (or the church reduces it), it is the way of life, a lifelong commitment that involves children and your families too.
12/24/11 2:11:25: UNkosiyazi: swallow your pride and stick by your man. dont worry about what your friends might say, they probably dont have a man that loves them or they cant keep a man.
12/24/11 2:13:27: NU17: So that he finds another woman while ndihleli mna.
12/24/11 2:13:54: NU17: Cz i this were me, he would have chased me out and taken my children.
12/24/11 2:14:04: UNkosiyazi: what do you mean? you want to compete?
12/24/11 2:15:50: NU17: i won't compete. I'm just saying if this were me, things would b very different
12/24/11 2:16:18: UNkosiyazi: remember, you are a mother of those children but you dont have a right to take them away from their father when their father is trying to save his marriage with you and also trying to give them more siblings.
12/24/11 2:17:48: UNkosiyazi: when you say so you infer that it should be a tit-for-tat situation.
12/24/11 2:20:52: UNkosiyazi: i'll suggest you go home and get serious advice from your elders, not your mother. you mother will condone you even if you are wrong.
12/24/11 2:21:16: UNkosiyazi: "forge"
12/24/11 12:36:05: UNkosiyazi: what are you reading these days?
12/24/11 12:39:28: NU17: Nothing hey. Been lazy.
12/24/11 12:45:26: UNkosiyazi: im disappointed in you. why?
12/24/11 12:52:55: NU17: Why?
12/24/11 12:53:59: UNkosiyazi: coz u hav bin prioritizing other things instead of your spiritual growth.
12/24/11 13:21:01: NU17: i really have...i let life get in the way

12/24/11 13:29:21: UNkosiyazi: you have children, you have a man, it is time to focus on your career now but not at the expense of your motherly and wife duties.

SUNNYSIDE

11/23/11 11:41:58: Sunnyside: A cucumber, an onion & a penis were talking about life.Cucumber:-"When I get big & hard they chop me up & toss me in a salad."Onion:-"You got it easy mate, when I get big & hard they skin me & drown me in vinegar."Penis:-"Lads, that's nothing compared to what I go thru when I get big & hard, they put a plastic bag over my head, shove me in a small, warm, damp cave & keep banging my head until I throw up & faint.!=))

11/23/11 11:44:46: UNkosiyazi: funny

11/23/11 23:21:18: UNkosiyazi: <media omitted>

11/23/11 23:21:28: UNkosiyazi: Thanksgiving

11/24/11 1:29:21: Sunnyside: Lolng interesting combination

11/24/11 3:55:51: Sunnyside: UMpongo usesibhedela samahlanya,Ä¶.
11/24/11 7:32:58: UNkosiyazi: hahaha...

11/24/11 21:20:17: UNkosiyazi: bottle after bottle till i get messed up.

11/24/11 21:57:28: UNkosiyazi: tell me, what's that song about Tkzee "ela ngwana wa ka..."?

11/24/11 23:08:39: Sunnyside: I'm sorry I don't listen to their music

11/24/11 23:16:48: UNkosiyazi: hahaha... that's an old skul track.

11/24/11 23:17:59: Sunnyside: Mybe I wasn't born

11/24/11 23:18:07: Sunnyside: Lol

11/24/11 23:18:29: UNkosiyazi: funny

11/26/11 1:24:23: UNkosiyazi: good morning!

11/26/11 6:29:34: Sunnyside: Whatup

11/26/11 10:13:40: UNkosiyazi: nuttin much...

11/26/11 10:13:56: UNkosiyazi: whatsup with you?

11/26/11 10:16:01: Sunnyside: We having I phatlo

11/26/11 10:16:57: UNkosiyazi: what is that?

11/26/11 10:18:10: Sunnyside: <media omitted>

11/26/11 10:20:29: UNkosiyazi: yummy... mail me one so i can partake too.

11/26/11 10:20:50: Sunnyside: Lol send me your e-mail lolng

11/26/11 10:21:32: UNkosiyazi: hah!

11/26/11 10:22:47: Sunnyside: Lol uyahhala

11/26/11 10:25:47: UNkosiyazi: uwena ongihhaliselayo.

11/26/11 10:26:18: Sunnyside: Nawe uhle wenzanjalo

11/26/11 10:30:14: UNkosiyazi: manje uyakhokhisela?

11/26/11 10:30:36: Sunnyside: Kancane lol

11/26/11 10:32:28: UNkosiyazi: hahaha...

11/26/11 10:33:11: Sunnyside: Usuku lwakho lukuphethe kanjan

11/26/11 10:33:40: UNkosiyazi: ima ngivuka, ngisasengubweni.

11/26/11 10:34:40: Sunnyside: Hawu ngalisikhathi?

11/26/11 10:34:43: Sunnyside: Why?

11/26/11 10:36:20: UNkosiyazi: ngilale after 3am.

11/26/11 10:37:22: Sunnyside: Cha bezikukhiphela

11/26/11 10:47:23: UNkosiyazi: ukube uyazi, bengihlalele umsebenzi.

11/26/11 10:48:27: Sunnyside: Ebusuku kangaka

11/26/11 10:49:01: UNkosiyazi: ukuhlupheka kodwa.

11/26/11 14:17:44: UNkosiyazi: uyamazi uPastor Mjosty? can you send me his tracks?

11/27/11 1:37:34: UNkosiyazi: ulale kanjani?

11/27/11 1:55:49: Sunnyside: To answer your question about umjosti yeah I do know him but I don't have his sermons.and the sleeping part I didn't cause my bf's place almost got broken into and on friday they broke into his car

11/27/11 2:25:04: UNkosiyazi: i hear u...

11/28/11 0:23:28: UNkosiyazi: goodmorning!
11/28/11 0:24:27: Sunnyside: Morning morning I'm good hope your well enjoy your day

11/28/11 0:26:11: UNkosiyazi: will do so after my sleep.

11/28/11 0:27:19: Sunnyside: Hawe futhi ?

11/28/11 0:28:04: UNkosiyazi: time is 00:28

11/28/11 0:28:47: Sunnyside: Lol my bad

11/29/11 1:04:58: UNkosiyazi: "i just cant believe that you've been sent to me from above. you're my angel of love. i cant wait to feel your sunshine..."
11/29/11 1:06:45: Sunnyside: Yoh there are so many house tracks maybe the artist will narrow the search and which genre of house deep/commercial

11/29/11 1:18:46: UNkosiyazi: im listenin to it while sippin Southern Comfort...

11/29/11 1:18:56: UNkosiyazi: <media omitted>

11/29/11 12:03:05: Sunnyside: A thief broke into a doctors surgery he saw a bowl full of dried meat then tasted a piece and realised that it was nice and salty,he sat down and ate as much as he could,later after he had finished all the biltong he looked upwards on the surgery door and saw written CIRCUMCISION ROOMX_X

11/29/11 12:16:12: UNkosiyazi: hahaha...
11/29/11 14:43:38: UNkosiyazi: http://www.realtor.com/blogs/2011/11/23/bruce-willis-lists-idaho-home-photos/

11/29/11 15:53:58: UNkosiyazi: send me a picture or two, just wanna see you.

11/29/11 15:56:47: Sunnyside: Just took this one now

11/29/11 15:57:17: Sunnyside: <media omitted>

11/29/11 15:59:05: UNkosiyazi: wow, you look immaculate.

11/29/11 15:59:42: Sunnyside: Lolng thanx I'm studying though

11/29/11 16:01:26: UNkosiyazi: thanks4sending. it's nice2c u without unnatural hair.
11/29/11 16:08:16: Sunnyside: Lol mxm Thursday at 9:30 and 11:30

11/29/11 16:10:55: UNkosiyazi: musa ukunxapha, iqiniso. ayikufaneli iwiggy.

11/29/11 16:11:16: UNkosiyazi: anyway, what are you writing?

11/29/11 16:19:51: Sunnyside: Lol I never wore a wig

11/29/11 16:20:05: Sunnyside: Research and comp. App

11/29/11 16:21:30: UNkosiyazi: what is that?

11/29/11 16:24:08: Sunnyside: Computer application

11/29/11 16:36:54: UNkosiyazi: cool

11/29/11 16:40:13: UNkosiyazi: <media omitted>

11/29/11 16:40:20: UNkosiyazi: detoxing...

11/29/11 16:54:59: Sunnyside: Ag your mad

11/29/11 16:56:41: UNkosiyazi: what do you mean: MAD?

11/29/11 16:56:56: UNkosiyazi: r u insultin me?

11/29/11 17:08:44: Sunnyside: You can't detox with that

11/29/11 20:10:15: UNkosiyazi: hah!

11/30/11 8:59:45: Sunnyside: A guy in a hurry used the ladies toilet in a
11/30/11 10:11:49: Sunnyside: At dinner a little boy offered to lead in prayer;
11/30/11 11:00:44: UNkosiyazi: pow! hah!
11/30/11 11:03:36: Sunnyside: Lol thanx

11/30/11 16:05:02: UNkosiyazi: Classic material indeed...
http://yourblackwoman.blogspot.com/2011/12/meet-sara-bartman-original-video-vixen.html#more

12/1/11 2:06:49: Sunnyside: A wife said to her doctor,"Doc my husband dick is so big everytime we have sex I feel it touching my heart,I swear he will kill me with it real soon if u don't do something",the doc said,"would u like me to cut off a inch or so off hubby's dick?" the woman jumped up & shouted,"Hell no Doc!!..are you crazy?..I want you to move my heart!!!

12/1/11 2:11:27: UNkosiyazi: hahaha... tji tji tji...

12/1/11 15:14:46: UNkosiyazi: A spiritually evolved woman understands the difference between chasing men and choosing a husband. The difference has a profound effect on the quality of life for her, her offspring and her community. Strong married couples build wealthy families which, in turn, build affluent communities. When the majority of babies are born to single individuals, or into marriages that don‚Äôt last, you can‚Äôt sustain an economically sound community. There is a lack of physical comfort because we are not pooling resources. People are fighting over child support and stretching one income among several households.

12/2/11 1:26:55: UNkosiyazi: how did you sleep?

12/2/11 1:32:02: Sunnyside: Morning I died - wena?

12/2/11 1:34:51: UNkosiyazi: died from what? from your paper izolo or u writin anada 1 namhlanje?

12/2/11 1:36:11: UNkosiyazi: im nice, just made my bed, about to rest. listening to my fav French rapper: Oxmo Puccino

12/2/11 1:36:42: Sunnyside: Nah I wrote then after the we had to move and that was the tiring part

12/2/11 1:38:35: UNkosiyazi: move to where?
12/2/11 1:39:25: Sunnyside: Moved in with who??

12/2/11 1:40:29: UNkosiyazi: isoka

12/2/11 1:42:04: Sunnyside: Lolng I don't do I vat en set

12/2/11 1:44:25: UNkosiyazi: good for your health.

12/2/11 1:46:08: Sunnyside: Lol and value

12/2/11 1:47:47: UNkosiyazi: especially VALUE. isimilo

12/2/11 1:49:30: Sunnyside: And chances of you getting married mancane

12/2/11 1:53:42: UNkosiyazi: hahaha...
12/2/11 1:54:19: Sunnyside: Lolng but was your intention to marry any of them?

12/2/11 1:55:47: UNkosiyazi: honestly, i wanna marry them but the issues, they dont quite take the fact that i want a unique living arrangements.

12/2/11 1:57:54: Sunnyside: Lolng no woman wants that unless kuse kandla

12/2/11 2:00:45: UNkosiyazi: what's "kandla"?

12/2/11 2:01:01: Sunnyside: Farms

12/2/11 2:01:17: UNkosiyazi: oh, Nkandla?

12/2/11 2:02:14: UNkosiyazi: actually, i want a farm- wanna live in a farm and herd cows, goats and chickens.

12/2/11 2:02:51: Sunnyside: Lolng hai bo - don't you wana urbanise yourself?

12/2/11 2:06:51: UNkosiyazi: city is not for me. life is hard in the urban space plus there are too many restrictions on what you can and cant do with your property (and money).

12/2/11 2:07:58: Sunnyside: So do your think you half spanish american wife would want ukuyohlala emafarm

12/2/11 2:09:02: UNkosiyazi: ifuna mina nokuba nami, uyongithola emafamu.

12/2/11 2:09:19: UNkosiyazi: meant: "ofuna".

12/2/11 2:10:18: Sunnyside: Tltltltltllt lolng maye lama conditions mina angeke

12/2/11 2:10:22: UNkosiyazi: angincengi mfazi or bafazi, i'll lead and those who want to follow, will follow.

12/2/11 2:10:56: UNkosiyazi: stakes is high.

12/2/11 2:11:28: Sunnyside: Lolng ha ha ha ha. Weeee msholozi maye uzuphethe lol ingane zabantu

12/2/11 2:14:56: UNkosiyazi: hah!

12/2/11 2:15:46: Sunnyside: What are those high stakes anyway?

12/2/11 2:16:24: UNKosiyazi: different strokes for different folks.
12/2/11 2:17:23: UNKosiyazi: stakes is high because now it is about DO or DIE. about making HARD DECISIONS.

12/2/11 2:18:03: Sunnyside: But amafarm is not an option though come on

12/2/11 2:18:35: UNkosiyazi: how about modernized mafamu?

12/2/11 2:19:33: Sunnyside: Amafarm ayohlala ayiwo

12/2/11 2:20:07: UNkosiyazi: filthy rich (i mean wealthy) people dont live in the city or suburbs but emafamu or so called ranches or estates.

12/2/11 2:20:51: UNkosiyazi: ...so they can have their horses, cows and stuff.

12/2/11 2:20:58: Sunnyside: So you planning on staying there for good

12/2/11 2:22:41: UNkosiyazi: want a vineyard, horses, cows, a lake, wattle and stuff.
12/2/11 2:23:41: Sunnyside: You can get those in cape

12/2/11 2:23:43: UNkosiyazi: i'll probably keep a one bedroom near a city or suburb to stay when im visiting the city.

12/2/11 2:23:58: Sunnyside: Usabi dolobha

12/2/11 2:24:10: UNkosiyazi: or in Mooi River or in California.

12/2/11 2:25:30: Sunnyside: Buya ekhaya baba

12/2/11 2:25:33: UNkosiyazi: angilisabi idolobha, ngiyalinyanya nje kuphela. ngiyindoda, angikwazi ukukhuza abantwana nomakhelwane bonke belakele.

12/2/11 2:26:08: UNkosiyazi: meant: "belalele".

12/2/11 2:26:28: Sunnyside: Stereotype sthandwa

12/2/11 2:26:50: UNkosiyazi: ive lived in Cape Town, i dont like it like that.

12/2/11 2:27:40: UNkosiyazi: im thinkin Argentina or Cameroon or California to raise all of my children.

12/2/11 2:27:44: Sunnyside: Uthanda kephi kanti

12/2/11 2:29:31: Sunnyside: Sho how many do you plan on having

12/2/11 2:31:02: UNkosiyazi: dont have a fixed namba but im gonna have a decent amount.

12/2/11 2:31:29: Sunnyside: How much is decent

12/2/11 2:32:54: UNkosiyazi: cant put an amount. as many as the powera that be allow.

12/2/11 2:33:13: UNkosiyazi: meant: "powers".

12/2/11 2:34:55: Sunnyside: Lolng hai you very interesting targets in life

12/2/11 2:36:13: UNkosiyazi: that is why i said: "honestly, i wanna marry them but the issues, they dont quite take the fact that i want a unique living arrangements."

12/2/11 2:37:05: Sunnyside: Yoh let me take a shower and start my day

12/2/11 2:37:30: UNkosiyazi: lemme see a nipple atleast.

12/2/11 2:38:04: Sunnyside: Lolng cant

12/2/11 2:38:14: UNkosiyazi: sweet talking to you, enjoy your day.

12/2/11 2:41:42: Sunnyside: You too

12/2/11 2:44:40: UNkosiyazi: ngiyazibongela Chibi, Mlambo omkhulu ongawelwa muntu.

12/2/11 13:40:12: Sunnyside: Hey

12/2/11 15:06:22: UNkosiyazi: hey

12/2/11 15:06:33: UNkosiyazi: <media omitted>

12/2/11 15:07:59: Sunnyside: Hawu mandla lohhu bhu olubhemayo

12/2/11 15:12:19: UNkosiyazi: hahaha...
12/2/11 15:13:36: Sunnyside: I've noticed hai ayikuhhishi lento?

12/2/11 15:17:14: UNkosiyazi: lutho

12/2/11 15:46:17: UNkosiyazi: <media omitted>

12/2/11 15:50:18: Sunnyside: Manje uhhogela konke

12/2/11 15:53:29: UNkosiyazi: cha

12/3/11 0:04:03: UNkosiyazi: mornin! is it a gud one or what?
12/3/11 15:35:19: UNkosiyazi: Lay down here beside me and we‚Äôll cruise the caravan
12/4/11 12:55:34: UNkosiyazi: <media omitted>

12/4/11 12:55:43: UNkosiyazi: howaz yo day?
12/4/11 12:56:45: Sunnyside: all good spending the weekend with my bf. What's happening ngalakho

12/4/11 12:57:37: UNkosiyazi: chillin, listenin to Bob Marley and blazin my cigars.

12/4/11 12:57:47: UNkosiyazi: <media omitted>

12/4/11 12:59:00: Sunnyside: Lolng again isn't there a law lapho states about smoking too much I think your turning into isitimelasama lahle lol

12/4/11 13:00:19: UNkosiyazi: <media omitted>

12/4/11 13:00:28: UNkosiyazi: hahaha...

12/4/11 13:01:45: Sunnyside: Manje lelo phakethe uliqheda after how long

12/4/11 13:02:23: UNkosiyazi: it will take me a month two smoke four cigars.

12/4/11 13:02:41: UNkosiyazi: meant: "to".

12/4/11 13:02:46: Sunnyside: Hai bo kanti lento ingakanani?

12/4/11 13:03:38: UNkosiyazi: ubhema ushiye uphinde ubheme ushiye, it's not like usikilidi.

12/4/11 13:04:17: UNkosiyazi: some of them you can only smoke them after eating a meal.

12/4/11 13:04:45: Sunnyside: Umsebenzi nje

12/4/11 13:06:01: UNkosiyazi: it's a great job, a hobby, a pastime activity.

12/4/11 13:07:18: UNkosiyazi: <media omitted>

12/4/11 13:07:37: UNkosiyazi: sengibekile for later on.

12/4/11 16:01:36: UNkosiyazi: sweet dreams.
12/4/11 18:18:51: UNkosiyazi: my snuff supply is getting depleted, can you mail me some more?

12/5/11 2:44:59: Sunnyside: What do you mean I'm lost

12/5/11 2:47:11: UNkosiyazi: hahaha...

12/5/11 2:47:39: Sunnyside: Uyabonake *esho edonsa ubuso*

12/5/11 2:48:30: UNkosiyazi: i nid snuff (ugwayi wamakhala), usuyangiphelela. ngithumelele amadosha amabili noma amathathu.

12/5/11 2:50:01: Sunnyside: Lolng mxm ngize ngizixake ngovalo

12/5/11 2:50:03: Sunnyside: Oho

12/5/11 2:51:24: UNkosiyazi: oho, ini?

12/5/11 2:52:18: Sunnyside: Chaphela mina ngicabanga into ebalulekile mawuthi sekuyancipha

12/5/11 2:52:57: UNkosiyazi: into ebaluleke njengani?

12/5/11 2:53:42: Sunnyside: Mengithi usho umshini wakho ukuthi usuyancipha

12/5/11 2:57:38: UNkosiyazi: hahaha... kunokuthi wande ungancipha kanjani? kusamele usebenze wenze izingane.

12/5/11 3:04:48: Sunnyside: Lolng hai phela k'dala wacgina uku shisa impepha so abakini bayaku-punisher

12/5/11 3:47:02: UNkosiyazi: ukube uyazi, bengiyishisa zolo lokhu.

12/5/11 6:00:28: Sunnyside: Ngoba ayikho lapho , uyithathephi?

12/5/11 10:29:56: UNkosiyazi: got lots of it from SA.

12/5/11 10:31:09: Sunnyside: Lolng abathi yinsangu?

12/5/11 10:32:22: UNkosiyazi: lutho. bayayazi insangu injani.

12/5/11 11:03:33: Sunnyside: Manje bayibizani ke?

12/5/11 12:09:37: UNkosiyazi: the Native Americans (so called Red Indians) have something like impepho too.

12/5/11 12:11:28: Sunnyside: Oooh ja - I thought you used china sticks lolng

12/5/11 12:12:24: UNkosiyazi: hahaha... uzamlandela!
12/5/11 12:13:09: UNkosiyazi: question is: uzongiposela ugwayi wezalukazi?

12/5/11 12:19:08: UNkosiyazi: As in the stuff in the blue and yellow container?

12/5/11 12:35:10: Sunnyside: Where do I get that stuff konje

12/5/11 12:36:13: UNkosiyazi: Shoprite, tuckshops, Spar, PicknPay, etc...

12/5/11 12:36:18: UNkosiyazi: i use it to talk to my grandmothers when i leave the house or wherever i am. it's like a rosary or thusby that reminds me to pray (talk) to my caregivers (ancestors).
12/5/11 12:37:56: UNkosiyazi: remember, even when you drink your fav beverages to spill some for them too.
12/5/11 12:49:27: UNkosiyazi: listen and learn, you gonna be a mother and a wife someday, hopefully. you gonna be a granny, God willing. you definately gonna be an ancestor, you dont have a choice.

12/6/11 23:23:54: UNkosiyazi: i like this Luther song:
Wednesday, December 7, 2011
12/7/11 11:18:40: UNkosiyazi: seems like it is going to be a good
show for the Emerging Black Middle Class on SABC1:
12/7/11 12:21:29: UNkosiyazi: Philadelphia D.A. Drops Death Penalty
Against Mumia Abu-Jamal
12/7/11 12:30:53: UNkosiyazi: FREE MUMIA!
12/7/11 20:20:32: UNkosiyazi: <media omitted>

12/7/11 20:31:19: UNkosiyazi: i did a film about President Zuma
before he came into power, and i have never showed it to anyone. im
wondering if time is right for me to release it now or should i wait
until end of next year?
12/7/11 23:17:06: Sunnyside: Lolng kwaaaaa lolng I think now is
perfect

12/7/11 23:18:31: UNkosiyazi: how come?

12/7/11 23:19:06: Sunnyside: Lolng with tha naming and shaming I
thunk it would do justice

12/7/11 23:22:51: UNkosiyazi: how about i wait until next year
September or October?

12/7/11 23:23:21: Sunnyside: Lolng nah that won't fit lol now is the
time

12/7/11 23:26:43: UNkosiyazi: you still not saying / justifying WHY
NOW?

12/7/11 23:30:54: Sunnyside: His term has come to end

12/7/11 23:36:44: UNkosiyazi: cool

12/7/11 23:57:51: UNkosiyazi: <media omitted>

12/7/11 23:57:59: UNkosiyazi: a teaser... hah!

12/8/11 0:13:38: UNkosiyazi: <media omitted>

12/8/11 0:24:50: UNkosiyazi: <media omitted>

12/8/11 1:58:15: UNkosiyazi: ps: the Children's Book is ready, for now it is just art (drawings) with date stamps and titles.
12/8/11 1:59:39: UNkosiyazi: ...you should get a copy for your young cousins (nieces and nephews).

12/8/11 2:26:00: UNkosiyazi: some dreams stay dreams and others dreams come true.

12/8/11 2:28:07: UNkosiyazi: Liquid Deep says: "...never let go of your dreams. no matter how hard it may seem."
12/10/11 0:48:24: UNkosiyazi: <media omitted>

12/10/11 0:48:28: UNkosiyazi: gudmornin!

12/10/11 12:52:21: UNkosiyazi: AmaPantsula Ajabulile = Professor ft Kabelo
12/10/11 12:59:20: UNkosiyazi: you like Ungazoba Serious = Big NUZ?

12/11/11 13:19:26: UNkosiyazi: <media omitted>

12/11/11 13:20:49: Sunnyside: Sorry haven't texed back was is a car accident a while back

12/11/11 13:27:20: UNkosiyazi: that's not good. how are you? what happened? when? are you okay?

12/11/11 13:28:44: Sunnyside: I'm okay now_where you headed ?

12/11/11 13:31:54: UNkosiyazi: to see someone.

12/11/11 13:32:40: UNkosiyazi: good to know you are okay, qaphela next time.

12/11/11 13:33:41: Sunnyside: Lol I will - please show me what you see I'm drooling over that vid

12/11/11 13:38:15: UNkosiyazi: hahaha... you have to come visit me and uzobona.

12/11/11 13:39:16: Sunnyside: If besihamba ngakhaso-banana ngabe kulula

12/11/11 13:41:52: UNkosiyazi: hahaha...

12/11/11 13:42:16: UNkosiyazi: <media omitted>

12/11/11 13:42:51: Sunnyside: I'm glad were on the same page lol

12/11/11 13:43:14: Sunnyside: Is it cold there?

12/11/11 13:43:38: UNkosiyazi: minus three degrees today.

12/11/11 13:45:49: Sunnyside: Are you for real ??? Kushisa kanje lana

12/11/11 13:46:52: UNkosiyazi: im for real, it's going to drop to minus eight tonite.

12/11/11 13:47:30: Sunnyside: Why is it winter?

12/11/11 13:48:39: UNkosiyazi: yebo

12/11/11 13:48:43: Sunnyside: <media omitted>

12/11/11 13:49:33: UNkosiyazi: niyabusa bo lapho, nibahle ninje!

12/11/11 13:49:35: Sunnyside: Gabi gabi siyabhukuda lana

12/11/11 13:50:39: UNkosiyazi: kuyoze kuqale ukufudumala kuthina by end of May.

12/11/11 13:52:16: Sunnyside: Wooh shame ngizo bhukuda on your behalf lol

12/11/11 13:53:30: UNkosiyazi: ngiyakucela, ungibeke entokozweni yakho Sthandwa sami!

12/11/11 13:54:05: Sunnyside: OHh I will dear I will

12/11/11 13:54:48: UNkosiyazi: ngiyabonga mina.

12/11/11 13:56:06: Sunnyside: So how's the christmas there?

12/11/11 14:02:44: UNkosiyazi: you know the ecitement, houses are decorated, sales all over the shops and internet, xmas trees galore.
12/11/11 14:03:37: Sunnyside: Nah,why did they change it

12/11/11 14:05:12: UNkosiyazi: ...they dont believe in Jesus anymore, they used him to control us and now that we are in control, the Zionist (Jews) who control the world dont want hear about Jesus.

12/11/11 14:06:21: Sunnyside: Nah I only heard about the money issue

12/11/11 14:08:56: UNkosiyazi: yeah, that is what's up. children r not even allowed to pray in schools anymore.

12/11/11 14:09:02: Sunnyside: In bed

12/11/11 14:09:27: UNkosiyazi: ...with who?
12/11/11 14:09:28: Sunnyside: The who do they pray to?

12/11/11 14:09:46: Sunnyside: Nah wrong text

12/11/11 14:10:18: UNkosiyazi: you know in school we used to sing and pray in assembly?

12/11/11 14:11:21: Sunnyside: Yeah but if they stop that there isn't a common religion

12/11/11 14:12:36: UNkosiyazi: true, im glad they are stopping it coz it used to offend some of us who dont believe in Jesus.

12/11/11 14:15:25: Sunnyside: Its not about that - look at It kanjena its not about jesus per say just about having uniform within the school

12/11/11 14:19:14: UNkosiyazi: why then not use Islam, Judaism, Bhuddism, Shembe, etc? why only use Xstianity, forcing everyone to conform to a uniform system that doesnt represent them? hhe?

12/11/11 14:21:54: Sunnyside: Cause its the only common

12/11/11 14:22:46: UNkosiyazi: says who?

12/11/11 14:23:40: Sunnyside: Me_ to how many countries would you go to and people would know shembe??

12/11/11 14:25:39: UNkosiyazi: you cant talk democracy and freedom of expression and still force people to go against what is foreign to them. those who are Shembe or Rasta or Islam or Xstian should be allowed to express themselves freely.

12/11/11 14:26:34: Sunnyside: True that's why accommodation is made for such on the school curriculum

12/11/11 14:29:49: UNkosiyazi: okay, we are saying the same thing.

12/11/11 14:31:13: Sunnyside: Thank you

12/11/11 14:58:09: UNkosiyazi: ulale kahle.

12/11/11 17:14:19: UNkosiyazi: <media omitted>

12/12/11 1:10:05: UNkosiyazi: how did you sleep?
12/12/11 1:40:11: Sunnyside: I slept alright_ how was your visit?

12/12/11 9:26:22: UNkosiyazi: that is gud to know, ive jus got up to. thankful for another new day to learn or do something new.

12/12/11 9:30:42: UNkosiyazi: it's minus six degrees outside.

12/12/11 9:31:44: Sunnyside: <media omitted>

12/12/11 9:31:48: Sunnyside: At 27degrees hoty

12/12/11 9:35:52: UNkosiyazi: oh, very nice. lucky you.

12/12/11 9:38:27: Sunnyside: Lol

12/12/11 10:06:15: UNkosiyazi: time's a wastin!
12/12/11 10:13:20: UNkosiyazi: it inspires me this Erykah Badu song:
12/12/11 10:14:20: Sunnyside: Don't you you _window sit?

12/12/11 10:16:33: UNkosiyazi: love the video, was watchin it on Friday.

12/12/11 10:18:14: Sunnyside: Please send it to me if you have

12/12/11 10:19:20: UNkosiyazi: hahaha... video or the song?
12/12/11 10:20:24: Sunnyside: The song or both?

12/12/11 10:21:28: UNkosiyazi: funny.
12/12/11 10:53:31: UNkosiyazi: in my dream last night, a woman was teaching me some deep doctrine and showing me some signs: i dont really recollect it all but i believe it was a sign of things to come that i will learn.

12/12/11 11:01:47: Sunnyside: Here's my new e-mail address_
lihle.Mlambo@yahoo.com

12/12/11 11:03:48: UNkosiyazi: cool

12/12/11 13:54:08: UNkosiyazi: Meet Sara Bartman: The Original Video
Vixen
12/12/11 13:57:47: Sunnyside: Kwl thanx

12/13/11 10:13:25: UNkosiyazi: are you going to mail me snuff?

12/13/11 15:11:02: UNkosiyazi: before you lay yourself down to sleep
tonight, know that im glad i know you and wish you well in all your
dreams.

12/13/11 22:53:31: UNkosiyazi: "To just spend all my time
12/14/11 3:28:30: UNkosiyazi: <media omitted>

12/14/11 3:28:36: UNkosiyazi: five Corona's, im feeling nice.

12/14/11 3:48:46: UNkosiyazi: anyway, im excited coz i re-started
(resumed) my Zulu novel today.

12/14/11 4:10:08: UNkosiyazi: im attacking Heineken now, cant stop,

12/14/11 4:10:08: UNkosiyazi: <media omitted>

12/14/11 4:15:21: UNkosiyazi: <media omitted>

12/14/11 5:05:05: UNkosiyazi: what am i trying to prove? it's five in
the morning, im off to sleep.

12/14/11 7:03:50: Sunnyside: Hey hey sorry over slept

12/14/11 7:04:15: Sunnyside: What's the title of your book?

12/14/11 11:15:57: UNkosiyazi: i dont know yet.

12/14/11 11:16:38: Sunnyside: Lol what was the last one?

12/14/11 11:17:14: UNkosiyazi: which one?

12/14/11 11:18:26: Sunnyside: "anyway, im excited coz i re-started (resumed) my Zulu novel today."

12/14/11 11:20:48: UNkosiyazi: that's the one i am not sure of its title, yet.

12/14/11 11:21:57: Sunnyside: Lol what's it about?

12/14/11 11:23:19: UNkosiyazi: ...about relationships with women.

12/14/11 11:26:45: Sunnyside: Call it mas'hlekisane cause that's what happens whens when you start a relationship with a woman

12/14/11 11:29:05: UNkosiyazi: want an English title to grab attention of Black Middle Class whom im addressing.

12/14/11 11:29:29: Sunnyside: But its in Zulu

12/14/11 11:29:54: UNkosiyazi: yes, suburb Zulu.

12/14/11 14:48:19: UNkosiyazi: <media omitted>

12/14/11 14:49:28: Sunnyside: Ingwitshikwebu

12/14/11 14:50:18: UNkosiyazi: what about ingwijikhwebu?

12/14/11 14:50:18: Sunnyside: The title for your book

12/14/11 14:50:50: UNkosiyazi: title will be in English.

12/14/11 14:51:27: Sunnyside: Anywhu what does the name mean?

12/14/11 14:52:16: UNkosiyazi: sudden change of mind or heart or behaviour.

12/14/11 14:54:50: UNkosiyazi: Lrence Molefe already made a Zulu book titled INGWIJIKHWEBU in 1989.

12/14/11 14:55:00: UNkosiyazi: Lawrence

12/14/11 14:55:24: Sunnyside: Oh nowonder

12/17/11 22:05:05: UNkosiyazi: <media omitted>

12/19/11 1:20:54: UNkosiyazi: ...dont tell me you are still sleepin! rise and shine, it's a new day. enjoy it.
12/19/11 1:44:21: UNkosiyazi: im just watchin a program on CNN about marriage. they say in 1960 marriages were at 80% and last year they were at 41%. people prefer to co-habit now because the institution of marriage has been reduced to money, commodity and liability. evri one is pushing for a career before family. men prefer to marry one another these days.
12/19/11 1:46:18: UNkosiyazi: ive concluded that for me, im just gonna find someone who just wanna put family before career. there turn to be unnecessary competition when both r pushing career coz family (children) get compromised under the guise of "children are expensive".

12/19/11 1:47:13: Sunnyside: Wow I have a feeling you support that part

12/19/11 1:50:29: UNkosiyazi: which part?

12/19/11 1:53:00: Sunnyside: Cohabiting

12/19/11 1:57:47: UNkosiyazi: no cohabiting for me, thank you.

12/19/11 1:58:53: Sunnyside: Lol phela wena uthanda abafazi

12/19/11 2:05:10: UNkosiyazi: im a man and i cant share a room with a female.

12/19/11 2:05:32: UNkosiyazi: it is silly, a man wants a lot of children and wants their mother to be there for them (housewife).
12/19/11 2:10:31: UNkosiyazi: im a hard man, traditional and cultured. no way im going to do western marriage. im going traditional. she will not only marry me but my family also. if she cant get along with them, she'll have to ship out. leave my grannies children behind.
12/19/11 2:27:57: UNkosiyazi: ps: the CNN guy is crying over the fact that Kobe Bryant's wife is gonna part with half of Kobe's millions, joint custody of the children and alimony.
12/19/11 2:31:49: UNkosiyazi: traditional marriage is the way to protect the interests of the children.

12/19/11 2:32:12: Sunnyside: How do you mean?

12/19/11 2:32:57: UNkosiyazi: what do you mean: "how do i mean?"

12/19/11 2:33:55: Sunnyside: When you say traditional marriage protects the childrens interests

12/19/11 2:37:16: UNkosiyazi: when parents divorce, the children stay at home since they belong to the man's family. if she wants to stay with her children, kumele awubambe ushisa. where is she going nezingane zendoda?
12/19/11 2:39:40: Sunnyside: But I think its just how you as an individual feel about your arrangement and yes I would want half of your property masinezingane

12/19/11 2:46:05: UNkosiyazi: what do you want to do with my property? my brothers are the ones to look after my property when im gone, not umfazi. they look after my property and children until my male children are grown ukuvusa umuzi wami (uyise wabo).

12/19/11 22:36:23: UNkosiyazi: im still feelin this Drake track:
12/19/11 22:36:53: UNkosiyazi: Patience is a Virtue that is only possessed by a few.

12/19/11 23:11:52: UNkosiyazi: i feel creative juices tonight so lemme share a piece i've just thought about:
12/20/11 13:22:38: UNkosiyazi: <media omitted>

12/20/11 14:43:05: UNkosiyazi: before i forget and get caught up, lemme say: enjoy your festive season (in Zulu it's called Ishwama / feast of the first fruits or harvest)!

12/21/11 4:01:15: UNkosiyazi: <media omitted>

12/21/11 20:09:50: UNkosiyazi: <media omitted>

12/21/11 23:41:19: UNkosiyazi: <media omitted>

12/22/11 0:10:51: UNkosiyazi: i love sleeping on the floor...

12/22/11 0:18:34: Sunnyside: Morning_why?

12/22/11 0:22:29: UNkosiyazi: it rests and massages my body...
12/23/11 1:17:51: UNkosiyazi: here is the link to children art book by my kids:
http://www.amazon.com/gp/aw/d/B006P16D1I/ref=redir_mdp_mobile
12/23/11 1:34:27: Sunnyside: How old is your kid?

12/23/11 1:39:46: UNkosiyazi: which one?

12/23/11 1:40:10: Sunnyside: Lol the 1 who wrote the book

12/23/11 1:41:04: UNkosiyazi: hahaha... six years old

12/23/11 1:41:27: Sunnyside: Kanti bangakhi?

12/23/11 1:42:31: UNkosiyazi: children are wealth to me, cant disclose how much im worth.

12/23/11 1:43:17: Sunnyside: Come on

12/23/11 1:44:26: UNkosiyazi: excuse me but when it comes to children, im very protective. over protective.

12/23/11 1:44:49: Sunnyside: Your just disclosing the number

12/23/11 1:45:21: UNkosiyazi: you wanna have kids with me?

12/23/11 1:45:36: Sunnyside: Nah I'm good thanx

12/23/11 1:46:41: UNkosiyazi: exactly, that's why we are not gonna discuss specifics about them in their absence.

12/23/11 1:47:47: UNkosiyazi: im a private man.

12/23/11 1:48:47: Sunnyside: K

12/23/11 1:49:55: Sunnyside: Then why would I share that address cause all I know is its your kid who did it and nothing else?

12/23/11 1:53:25: UNkosiyazi: you'll share the address (link) because you support Art. besides, you asked me about the Author and i answered you. i choose not to entertain questions about me and how many kids i have and with which women- to me those are "specifics" that dont share light about the author.

12/23/11 1:55:30: UNkosiyazi: no disrespect, respect and understand that im in showbiz and im a parent so like a hen, i have to protect the chicks with my wings.

12/23/11 1:55:58: UNkosiyazi: the book is titled: CHICKENS AND GOATS

12/23/11 2:00:53: Sunnyside: Gosh golly_you make sound like a gossip column journalist

12/23/11 2:03:28: UNkosiyazi: hahaha... i still love you.

12/23/11 2:03:45: UNkosiyazi: please support it, rate it and jot a review while at it... much appreciated.
12/23/11 3:00:17: UNkosiyazi: AS I LAY ME DOWN TO SLEEP, WORDS FROM YASIIN BEY (AN ARTIST FORMERLY KNOWN AS MOS DEF) RINGS IN MY EARS WHEN HE SAYS:
12/23/11 9:24:58: UNkosiyazi: i had a gud sleep... woke up thinking:
12/23/11 10:18:41: UNkosiyazi: <media omitted>

12/23/11 10:18:45: UNkosiyazi: make time to read this. his company owns LVMH (Louis Vutton, Hennessy, Moet), Cartier, Alfred Dunhill, etc...
12/24/11 1:08:35: UNkosiyazi: <media omitted>

12/24/11 1:31:27: UNkosiyazi: Kanye West: "...50 told me go 'head switch the style up
12/24/11 1:32:17: UNkosiyazi: Rick Ross: ambition is priceless, it's in my vein.

12/24/11 11:06:14: UNkosiyazi: <media omitted>

12/24/11 11:07:29: UNkosiyazi: you like my smoothie?

12/24/11 11:08:52: Sunnyside: Hey_smoothie?

12/24/11 11:30:24: UNkosiyazi: hey baby!

12/24/11 12:36:47: UNkosiyazi: <media omitted>

12/24/11 12:36:54: UNkosiyazi: what are you reading these days?

12/24/11 15:38:30: Sunnyside: Nun much its holidays

12/24/11 15:41:43: UNkosiyazi: wow, you only read when it is skultym? how about for your personal enrichment?

12/24/11 15:48:52: Sunnyside: Yep don't have time during fedtives

12/24/11 15:48:58: Sunnyside: Festives

12/24/11 16:05:24: UNkosiyazi: hahaha...

MIDRAND

11/7/11 11:15:13: Midrand: I guess im jus really tired of having to read ur msgs bout women only being gud nough to bear children n nuting else, how u make men sound lyk women wuld seize to exsist widout dem.

11/7/11 11:17:32: Midrand: well excuse me fr grwing up in a home whr african traditions n rituals was not da main topic at da dnr table

11/7/11 11:24:52: Midrand: So yes im really tired of hearing bout all dis, i actually have real issues dat affect me so forgive for not responding rantings bout culture n anyting dats got to do wid it

11/8/11 12:18:41: UNkosiyazi: note taken...
11/8/11 13:47:36: Midrand: Wat i need n want frm u i knw dat u culd never give me caus u(

11/8/11 13:48:15: Midrand: U've made it very clear dat its not an option

11/8/11 13:53:58: UNkosiyazi: you need / want me to leave you alone?

11/8/11 13:55:15: UNkosiyazi: just say it...
11/11/11 11:11:30: UNkosiyazi: 11:11 11.11.11
11/11/11 1:12:31: UNkosiyazi: 1:11 11.11.11

11/11/11 3:18:49: Midrand: Wat does dat mean?

11/15/11 14:37:12: Midrand: I live in da past most of da tym n my journey feeld lyk an unwinding road, more to say, plenty to do but no help

11/15/11 14:37:48: Midrand: demons to fight n wars to win but its
hard

11/15/11 14:38:22: Midrand: tears n emotions always get in da way

11/15/11 14:38:51: Midrand: wat can man do against such trying timez

11/15/11 15:29:20: UNkosiyazi: interestin...

11/16/11 2:00:49: UNkosiyazi: my upcoming Portuguese film...
11/17/11 16:12:28: UNkosiyazi: im thinkin bout SA.

11/18/11 21:14:54: UNkosiyazi: missing amawings...

11/18/11 21:55:45: UNkosiyazi: 4edbdce12f556798fe49937befd19288.jpg
<attached>

11/18/11 21:55:50: UNkosiyazi: my food (rooibos tea, wings, rice,
potatoes w/Mayo) is ready.

11/20/11 3:29:02: UNkosiyazi: "Girls, I ask em do they smoke?
11/20/11 20:16:39: UNkosiyazi: 994b073485dd08620ad8745fd3c08a9a.jpg
<attached>

11/21/11 1:17:47: UNkosiyazi: Same Ole Love: Anita Baker
11/21/11 17:51:24: UNkosiyazi: you know Midrand, waz thinkin&thisiz
what i was thinkin:
11/21/11 22:40:51: Midrand: you know Midrand, waz thinkin&thisiz what
i was thinkin:
11/21/11 22:44:32: Midrand: Hey

11/21/11 22:44:57: UNkosiyazi: hi!

11/21/11 22:45:05: Midrand: i thot dat u didnt blv in 1

11/21/11 22:45:05: Midrand: Wow

11/21/11 22:45:06: Midrand: love

11/21/11 22:45:44: Midrand: but wat u wrote is really ....

11/21/11 22:45:51: Midrand: im speechless

11/21/11 22:46:01: UNkosiyazi: everything i do or say: it's about love.

11/21/11 22:47:11: UNkosiyazi: i have lots of love, sincere love. you know why? because im a man of my words.

11/22/11 9:19:08: Midrand: I miss talking to you

11/22/11 9:22:19: Midrand: its just dat i got really tired of reading da stuff u say bout women n mens double standards

11/22/11 9:23:20: Midrand: i've jus been feeling really hurt lately n da las ting i wanted to talk bout was human behavr n culture

11/22/11 9:48:45: UNkosiyazi: i hear you.
11/23/11 6:53:31: UNkosiyazi: Girls, I ask em do they smoke?
11/23/11 7:49:08: UNkosiyazi: is there a way you can get me the track titled JIKWA IMALI by Magesh (Tokollo)?

11/23/11 11:15:16: Midrand: Nope

11/23/11 11:15:39: Midrand: i dnt listen to dat kind of music

11/23/11 11:15:59: Midrand: n i dnt knw anyone dat does

11/23/11 11:17:24: UNkosiyazi: i hear you.

11/23/11 23:22:03: UNkosiyazi: Thanksgiving

11/24/11 10:32:04: Midrand: Did u have fun

11/24/11 10:40:25: UNkosiyazi: im still having fun baby, wish you were here.

11/24/11 10:41:34: Midrand: Mayb nxt yr

11/24/11 10:41:41: Midrand: how bout dat

11/24/11 10:42:17: Midrand: Im glad dat u having fun ,ò∫

11/24/11 10:43:04: UNkosiyazi: yeah, we can work on next year.

11/24/11 21:19:49: UNkosiyazi: bottle after bottle till i get messed up.

11/24/11 21:57:35: UNkosiyazi: tell me, what's that song about Tkzee "ela ngwana wa ka..."?

11/26/11 1:24:48: UNkosiyazi: good morning!

11/26/11 2:26:59: UNkosiyazi: i waz callin to say: Hello!

11/26/11 2:27:54: Midrand: hello my angel

11/26/11 2:28:21: Midrand: arent u suppose to b in bed by now

11/26/11 2:29:09: UNkosiyazi: im in bed and im just up thinkin...

11/26/11 2:29:54: Midrand: Lol

11/26/11 2:29:56: Midrand: ok

11/26/11 2:30:11: Midrand: wat u tinking bout

11/26/11 2:31:16: UNkosiyazi: im thinkin about my dreams and wishes.

11/26/11 2:40:30: Midrand: Ok

11/26/11 2:59:37: UNkosiyazi: love without limit

11/26/11 9:14:27: Midrand: I thot dat u didnt blv in love

11/26/11 10:14:43: UNkosiyazi: love moves everything around me.

11/26/11 10:19:08: Midrand: Lol

11/26/11 10:19:43: Midrand: u sure do lyk to mess wid my mind neh

11/26/11 10:21:12: UNkosiyazi: i aint playing tricks / games with you.

11/27/11 1:38:06: UNkosiyazi: how did you sleep?

11/27/11 1:42:00: Midrand: Hey

11/27/11 1:42:19: Midrand: i slept very well

11/27/11 1:42:43: Midrand: Im jus still very tired

11/27/11 1:44:15: UNkosiyazi: you're tired from sleeping or sleeping (resting) got you tired?

11/27/11 1:46:50: Midrand: Not enough rest

11/28/11 0:23:39: UNkosiyazi: goodmorning!
11/29/11 0:41:48: UNkosiyazi: hope you slept well.

11/29/11 1:04:14: UNkosiyazi: "i just cant believe that you've been sent to me from above. you're my angel of love. i cant wait to feel your sunshine..."
11/29/11 1:20:04: UNkosiyazi: im listenin to it while sippin Southern Comfort...

11/29/11 3:08:22: Midrand: n u?

11/29/11 3:08:22: Midrand: I slept well thanx

11/29/11 3:08:42: Midrand: How did u sleep?

11/29/11 3:09:10: Midrand: I dnt knw dat house song

11/29/11 8:18:57: UNkosiyazi: just got up.
11/29/11 13:39:32: Midrand: Once upon a time there was an island where all the feelings lived; Happiness, Sadness, Knowledge, and all the others......, including Love.
11/29/11 13:40:17: Midrand: Sumting to read to yr kids

11/29/11 14:06:20: UNkosiyazi: immaculate.

11/29/11 14:07:40: UNkosiyazi: kids got a book coming out on Xmas, im busy doing final touches (edits). it's a children's book.

11/29/11 14:09:53: UNkosiyazi: i want the kids to be their own employers. i worked with them when i was in SA in August. they are excited about it, so am i.

11/29/11 14:43:28: UNkosiyazi: http://www.realtor.com/blogs/2011/11/23/bruce-willis-lists-idaho-home-photos/

11/29/11 15:52:42: UNkosiyazi: send me a picture or two, just wanna see you.

11/29/11 16:42:01: UNkosiyazi: detoxing...

11/29/11 22:32:16: UNkosiyazi: just thinkin, maybe it's the Heineken, i dont know but this i kno:
11/30/11 3:06:26: Midrand: Good morning

11/30/11 3:06:45: Midrand: i really do miss you

11/30/11 7:58:02: UNkosiyazi: good morning it is indeed

11/30/11 16:05:22: UNkosiyazi: Classic material indeed...
http://yourblackwoman.blogspot.com/2011/12/meet-sara-bartman-
original-video-vixen.html#more

12/1/11 10:14:44: UNkosiyazi: cute

12/1/11 10:18:12: Midrand: Lol

12/1/11 10:18:16: Midrand: cute

12/1/11 10:19:06: Midrand: is dat all u can say

12/1/11 10:20:39: UNkosiyazi: Black angel

12/1/11 12:26:34: Midrand: Why black angel

12/1/11 12:56:29: UNkosiyazi: because Black is beatiful and Black
females are Angelic.

12/1/11 12:57:46: UNkosiyazi: ...White females want you to fall from
grace when they define what is femininity / beauty / womanhood.

12/1/11 12:59:09: Midrand: U sure do have a way wid words

12/1/11 13:27:22: Midrand: My heart aches, my body yearns n my senses
want u

12/1/11 13:27:57: Midrand: Can you write sumting frm dat?

12/1/11 14:13:09: UNkosiyazi: how about you scribble something.
12/1/11 14:13:53: Midrand: Dnt b lyk dat

12/1/11 14:15:21: UNkosiyazi: lyk how Mntwana.

12/1/11 14:15:25: UNkosiyazi: ?

12/1/11 14:23:32: Midrand: U lyk doing dat

12/1/11 14:24:11: Midrand: i want u to lie to me wid ur wordplay

12/1/11 14:43:06: UNkosiyazi: talk about fantasy- hahaha...
12/1/11 14:48:08: Midrand: Ok cul

12/1/11 14:48:37: Midrand: i hope dat i can hear u dis tym

12/1/11 14:49:40: Midrand: Please write sumting

12/1/11 14:49:52: Midrand: well sumting for me

12/1/11 14:50:18: Midrand: sumting really beautiful

12/1/11 14:50:36: Midrand: pleeeeeease

12/1/11 14:59:52: UNkosiyazi: hah!
12/1/11 15:02:58: Midrand: I feel really undesirable ryt now

12/1/11 15:03:57: Midrand: n it wuld make me happy if u wuld seduce me wid ur words

12/1/11 15:05:41: UNkosiyazi: who made you feel "undesirable"?

12/1/11 15:06:47: UNkosiyazi: a church in Kentucky bans interracial couples.

12/1/11 15:08:29: UNkosiyazi: pick up the phone

12/1/11 15:14:35: UNkosiyazi: A spiritually evolved woman understands the difference between chasing men and choosing a husband. The difference has a profound effect on the quality of life for her, her offspring and her community. Strong married couples build wealthy families which, in turn, build affluent communities. When the

majority of babies are born to single individuals, or into marriages
that don‚Äôt last, you can‚Äôt sustain an economically sound
community. There is a lack of physical comfort because we are not
pooling resources. People are fighting over child support and
stretching one income among several households.

12/1/11 15:22:09: Midrand: I really hate it wen u speak lyk dat

12/1/11 15:22:45: Midrand: it makes me feel lyk such a pawn in ur
game

12/1/11 15:31:49: UNkosiyazi: i cant help or control how you feel
regarding certain things.

12/1/11 15:35:24: Midrand: Lol

12/1/11 15:35:28: Midrand: really

12/1/11 15:36:17: Midrand: u culd try n make me feel better

12/1/11 15:41:35: UNkosiyazi: im not gud at that...

12/1/11 15:42:08: UNkosiyazi: ...and when i try i usually insult.

12/1/11 15:47:28: Midrand: Ok....
12/1/11 16:15:32: Midrand: Wat does dat mean

12/1/11 16:16:00: UNkosiyazi: unity

12/1/11 16:16:23: Midrand: Lol

12/1/11 16:16:34: Midrand: Gudnyt

12/1/11 16:17:17: UNkosiyazi: sleep well

12/1/11 16:19:18: UNkosiyazi: im your

12/1/11 16:22:17: UNkosiyazi: you're my

12/2/11 1:26:03: UNkosiyazi: how did you sleep?

12/2/11 2:46:11: Midrand: I slept well thanx
12/2/11 2:48:31: UNkosiyazi: cool

12/2/11 2:49:04: Midrand: U shuld get to bed

12/2/11 2:50:54: UNkosiyazi: i am in bed, im just up thinking of ways
to realize my dreams.
12/3/11 0:04:23: UNkosiyazi: mornin! is it a gud one or what?
12/3/11 0:16:46: Midrand: Im at my cousins funeral

12/3/11 0:16:57: Midrand: Cnt really chat

12/3/11 0:17:55: UNkosiyazi: okay

12/3/11 15:33:57: UNkosiyazi: Lay down here beside me and we'll
cruise the caravan
12/4/11 12:56:36: UNkosiyazi: howaz yo day?
12/4/11 16:00:21: UNkosiyazi: sweet dreams.
12/4/11 18:19:04: UNkosiyazi: my snuff supply is getting depleted,
can you mail me some more?

12/5/11 12:14:28: UNkosiyazi: my snuff supply is getting depleted,
can you mail me some more?

12/5/11 12:18:22: UNkosiyazi: As in the stuff in the blue and yellow
container?

12/5/11 12:35:39: UNkosiyazi: i use it to talk to my grandmothers
when i leave the house or wherever i am. it's like a rosary or thusby
that reminds me to pray (talk) to my caregivers (ancestors).
12/5/11 12:37:43: UNkosiyazi: remember, even when you drink your fav
beverages to spill some for them too.

12/5/11 12:49:19: UNkosiyazi: listen and learn, you gonna be a mother and a wife someday, hopefully. you gonna be a granny, God willing. you definately gonna be an ancestor, you dont have a choice.

12/5/11 12:50:33: Midrand: I really dnt knw wat u want me to say

12/5/11 12:52:15: UNkosiyazi: answer the question: yes or no. will you send me some snuff?

12/5/11 12:53:37: Midrand: Pls dnt ask me to do dat

12/5/11 12:54:27: Midrand: i really dnt want to caus i happen to tink dat da stuff is disgusting

12/5/11 12:58:07: UNkosiyazi: dont be judgmental and critical.
12/5/11 13:00:25: Midrand: Im not, i jus dnt wanna do it hence da silence

12/5/11 13:00:59: UNkosiyazi: fair enough. thanks for responding.

12/6/11 13:30:23: Midrand: If wrote letters to u everyday

12/6/11 13:30:42: Midrand: Wuld u write back?

12/6/11 13:32:14: UNkosiyazi: wuld i write back to you "everyday"?

12/6/11 13:34:15: Midrand: Lol

12/6/11 13:34:33: Midrand: trust u to ask me dat

12/6/11 13:34:57: Midrand: i really neva dispnt

12/6/11 13:35:04: Midrand: Lol

12/6/11 13:35:32: Midrand: do u always gave to keep ur guard up wid me?

12/6/11 13:39:23: UNkosiyazi: i asked u: do i have to write back to you "everyday"?

12/6/11 13:40:56: Midrand: Yes

12/6/11 13:41:06: Midrand: lol

12/6/11 13:42:49: UNkosiyazi: im not sure about that but im sure i can give it a try. right? how would i know unless i try it!

12/6/11 13:43:32: Midrand: Lol

12/6/11 13:44:03: UNkosiyazi: hahaha...

12/6/11 13:44:17: Midrand: Its ok my luv, was jus asking to see if u wuld go for it

12/6/11 13:45:17: UNkosiyazi: okay!

12/6/11 13:46:51: UNkosiyazi: you should write books (novels)... your mind is attune with it.

12/6/11 13:48:27: Midrand: Hell ni

12/6/11 13:48:33: Midrand: No

12/6/11 13:48:56: Midrand: I told g dat i dnt write anymore

12/6/11 13:49:27: UNkosiyazi: fair enough, let the talent (blessing) go to waste.

12/6/11 13:50:28: Midrand: üòí now u trying to make me feel guilty

12/6/11 13:51:38: Midrand: n besides if i had to start writting i wuldnt knw whr to start

12/6/11 13:52:02: UNkosiyazi: u r guilty for burying your talent on the ground.

12/6/11 13:53:08: UNkosiyazi: ...you begin where u left off when u used to write.

12/6/11 13:54:11: Midrand: Easier said dan done

12/6/11 13:58:01: UNkosiyazi: for crying out loud, just pick up a paper and pen and write about me, how i inspire you, how i confuse you, how we met, what you like and dont like about me, etc.
12/6/11 13:58:55: UNkosiyazi: go ahead and write, you have your work cut out for you.

12/6/11 14:00:45: Midrand: U sure do have da nerve to say dat

12/6/11 14:01:14: UNkosiyazi: to say what?

12/6/11 14:02:18: Midrand: Wat u jus watsapped now

12/6/11 14:04:56: UNkosiyazi: listen Midrand, im not your enemy. i care about you, especially about your survival and wuld like to be remembered by you as a guy who stopped at nuttin to push you to succeed.
12/6/11 23:22:59: UNkosiyazi: i like this Luther song:
Wednesday, December 7, 2011
12/7/11 11:19:01: UNkosiyazi: seems like it is going to be a good show for the Emerging Black Middle Class on SABC1:
12/7/11 12:21:16: UNkosiyazi: Philadelphia D.A. Drops Death Penalty Against Mumia Abu-Jamal
12/7/11 12:31:03: UNkosiyazi: FREE MUMIA!
12/7/11 20:31:31: UNkosiyazi: i did a film about President Zuma before he came into power, and i have never showed it to anyone. im wondering if time is right for me to release it now or should i wait until end of next year?
12/7/11 23:58:48: UNkosiyazi: a teaser... hah!

12/8/11 1:56:34: UNkosiyazi: ps: the Children's Book is ready, for now it is just art (drawings) with date stamps and titles.
12/8/11 2:00:08: UNkosiyazi: ...you should get a copy for your young cousins (nieces and nephews).

12/8/11 2:25:47: UNkosiyazi: some dreams stay dreams and others dreams come true.

12/8/11 2:28:14: UNkosiyazi: Liquid Deep says: "...never let go of your dreams. no matter how hard it may seem."
12/10/11 0:47:47: UNkosiyazi: gudmornin!

12/10/11 11:07:43: Midrand: Hey

12/10/11 11:09:11: Midrand: decided to do da ancestral ritual on da

12/10/11 11:09:12: Midrand: 31

12/10/11 11:09:26: Midrand: 31st of dec

12/10/11 11:46:33: UNkosiyazi: what made you decide such?

12/10/11 11:47:00: Midrand: Dnt knw

12/10/11 11:47:09: Midrand: u i guess

12/10/11 11:48:22: UNkosiyazi: it cant be me or anyone: really, what made u decide to do it?

12/10/11 11:50:04: Midrand: I dnt knw

12/10/11 11:50:36: Midrand: Lyk really i dnt

12/10/11 12:11:01: UNkosiyazi: anyway, im happy and support your decision(s).

12/10/11 12:51:31: UNkosiyazi: AmaPantsula Ajabulile = Professor ft Kabelo
12/10/11 12:58:58: UNkosiyazi: you like Ungazoba Serious = Big NUZ?

12/11/11 14:58:47: UNkosiyazi: ulale kahle

12/12/11 1:09:47: UNkosiyazi: how did you sleep?
12/12/11 3:21:15: Midrand: I slept well

12/12/11 3:21:24: Midrand: Gud morning

12/12/11 9:27:38: UNkosiyazi: that is gud to know, ive jus got up too. thankful for another new day to learn or do something new.

12/12/11 9:30:32: UNkosiyazi: it's minus six degrees outside.

12/12/11 10:01:07: Midrand: Wow

12/12/11 10:01:10: Midrand: ok

12/12/11 10:06:03: UNkosiyazi: time's a wastin!
12/12/11 10:13:32: UNkosiyazi: it inspires me this Erykah Badu song:
12/12/11 10:53:49: UNkosiyazi: in my dream last night, a woman was teaching me some deep doctrine and showing me some signs: i dont really recollect it all but i believe it was a sign of things to come that i will learn.
12/12/11 13:54:38: UNkosiyazi: Meet Sara Bartman: The Original Video Vixen
12/13/11 0:49:59: UNkosiyazi: it's nights like these that makes me desire you Midrand it's full moon and minus five degrees outside.

12/13/11 14:28:47: Midrand: Miss you
12/13/11 14:39:37: UNkosiyazi: miss you more!

12/13/11 15:09:08: UNkosiyazi: before you lay yourself down to sleep tonight, know that i love you and wish you well.

12/13/11 22:53:50: UNkosiyazi: "To just spend all my time
12/14/11 0:56:04: Midrand: Is dat a song

12/14/11 1:02:00: UNkosiyazi: do you like the words (message)?

12/14/11 3:26:59: UNkosiyazi: five Corona's, im feeling nice.

12/14/11 3:49:37: UNkosiyazi: anyway, im excited coz i re-started (resumed) my Zulu novel today.

12/14/11 4:08:39: UNkosiyazi: im attacking Heineken now, cant stop,

12/14/11 5:04:26: UNkosiyazi: what am i trying to prove? it's five in the morning, im off to sleep.

12/14/11 6:29:51: Midrand: U jus neva want to ansa my q

12/14/11 11:15:11: UNkosiyazi: yes, it is a song by Luther Vandross and Gregory Hines.

12/14/11 11:16:49: Midrand: I knew it

12/14/11 11:17:17: Midrand: U jus lyk doing dat

12/14/11 11:17:36: Midrand: Using other peeps words

12/14/11 11:18:12: UNkosiyazi: ...yes i do, they say things better than i could.

12/14/11 11:18:55: UNkosiyazi: in my world it is called: being inspired by others.

12/15/11 3:42:48: Midrand: I had a dream bout a goat n lamb together

12/15/11 3:43:40: Midrand: My sis says dat i mus which one to slauvh

12/15/11 3:43:53: Midrand: Slaughter

12/15/11 3:44:12: Midrand: Wat do u tink

12/15/11 5:40:35: UNkosiyazi: ...sounds like a good dream.

12/15/11 5:50:32: Midrand: So which one must i choose

12/15/11 6:22:05: UNkosiyazi: before i answer u, lemme pose a question: who are you doing the "work" for and why?

12/15/11 6:25:00: Midrand: I thot it was tym i said thanks to my ancestors

12/15/11 6:25:16: Midrand: Hence da ritual

12/15/11 6:26:07: Midrand: n plus get rid of all da bad luck dats around

12/15/11 6:29:32: UNkosiyazi: okay, answer this: was your mother or any of your primary ancestors ever brought home? do you think you belong to your father or mother?

12/15/11 6:30:18: Midrand: I belong to my mom

12/15/11 6:30:54: UNkosiyazi: remind me: was your mother married to your father or did he lobola her or did he claim you?

12/15/11 6:32:09: Midrand: He didnt do shit for me

12/15/11 6:33:52: UNkosiyazi: remind me: was your mother married to your father or did he lobola her?

12/15/11 6:50:38: Midrand: No he didnt do anything for het

12/15/11 6:50:45: Midrand: her

12/15/11 6:54:34: UNkosiyazi: was your mother or any of your primary ancestors ever brought home?

12/15/11 7:19:43: Midrand: My gran is married

12/15/11 7:22:31: UNkosiyazi: i mean: did you bring your mother home after the funeral (burial)?

12/15/11 7:23:14: Midrand: Wat do u mean

12/15/11 7:27:16: UNkosiyazi: ...was there work done to bring your mother home after her funeral / burial?

12/15/11 7:37:16: Midrand: Yes we did

12/15/11 7:37:39: Midrand: late las year round dis tym

12/15/11 7:44:08: UNkosiyazi: okay, i was gonna say if she wasnt brought home, you would have to bring her home before you do work involving her.
12/15/11 7:54:13: Midrand: N do wat wid it

12/19/11 1:21:35: UNkosiyazi: ...dont tell me you are still sleepin! rise and shine, it's a new day. enjoy it.
12/19/11 1:43:38: UNkosiyazi: im just watchin a program on CNN about marriage. they say in 1960 marriages were at 80% and last year they were at 41%. people prefer to co-habit now because the institution of marriage has been reduced to money, commodity and liability. evri one is pushing for a career before family. men prefer to marry one another these days.
12/19/11 1:45:55: UNkosiyazi: ive concluded that for me, im just gonna find someone who just wanna put family before career. there turn to be unnecessary competition when both r pushing career coz family (children) get compromised under the guise of "children are expensive".

12/19/11 2:28:20: UNkosiyazi: ps: the CNN guy is crying over the fact
that Kobe Bryant's wife is gonna part with half of Kobe's millions,
joint custody of the children and alimony.
12/19/11 2:31:28: UNkosiyazi: traditional marriage is the way to
protect the interests of the children.

12/19/11 2:47:41: UNkosiyazi: what does she want to do with my
property? my brothers are the ones to look after my property when im
gone, not umfazi. they look after my property and children until my
male children are grown ukuvusa umuzi wami (uyise wabo).

NYAKALLO

10/17/11 1:02:49: UNkosiyazi: Thuto Ke Senotlolo: Mahlathini &Mahotella Queens

10/17/11 13:24:20: UNkosiyazi: Germany (Jews) Reopens Nazi Cases.
10/17/11 13:59:55: UNkosiyazi: a debt to collect.
10/17/11 14:01:31: UNkosiyazi: allow me to school you briefly: the spirit of a murdered one cannot reunite with spirit of its ancestors unless justice (retribution / revenge) is done to pacify it.
10/17/11 14:03:12: Nyakallo: Ha?

10/17/11 14:03:48: UNkosiyazi: gospel news for you

10/17/11 14:50:46: Nyakallo: Okay! Say then that A murders B. Then A takes their own life! What happens to the spirit of B?

10/17/11 15:11:55: UNkosiyazi: first of all: A's spirit will be consumed or reject by the ancestors (gods) for committing suicide thus bringing B's spirit to rest.

10/17/11 16:06:12: UNkosiyazi: ...but A's people will have to lick the wounds of B's people.

10/17/11 16:07:52: UNkosiyazi: ...if the ancestors and gods rejects A's spirit, family members are then blanketed by this veil of darkness that will need a ceremony to remove.

10/17/11 17:47:07: UNkosiyazi: ANCIENT BANTU HISTORY: the Zulu Surgeons of 17th century and beyond: did things that the White men hasn't even dreamt of yet.

10/17/11 21:08:16: UNkosiyazi: space and time are one and the same thing.
10/17/11 21:38:32: UNkosiyazi: where in the Bible do they get this maths: Preacher man takes ten percent of gross, government comes and take its taxes, bills come and take almost everything. what am i left with?
10/18/11 2:45:24: UNkosiyazi: on a lighter note: been dreaming about the new "two door" Range Rover.

10/18/11 6:17:46: Nyakallo: Hi!

10/18/11 6:20:36: Nyakallo: Question of the day: y would your own ancestors reject u, when they know what has happened to u was not ur fault? Is the spirit meant to roam seeking revenge/retribution

10/18/11 9:00:34: UNkosiyazi: they'll reject you for disgrscing them, same way as a father will when her daughter falls pregnant outside of wedlock.
10/18/11 9:02:24: UNkosiyazi: ps: killing is a NO NO unless if it is self-defense or if it is against a dreaded enemy.
10/20/11 8:43:57: UNkosiyazi: Young Girls and the Dangers of the 'Booty Pose'.
10/20/11 12:28:08: UNkosiyazi: http://yourblackwoman.blogspot.com/2011/10/sojourner-marable-grimmett-young-girls.html

10/21/11 19:16:29: UNkosiyazi: in 2008 in South Africa: 54% Whites graduated with PhD's while Blacks were 13%. what a shame- we need KNOWLEDGE CREATORS. let us pursue high education &encourage others. Whites are going to rule and control us if we are not careful. our children should know from word go that the lowest level of education for them is PhD.

10/21/11 19:28:24: UNkosiyazi: come now!
10/22/11 23:48:44: UNkosiyazi: the sun goes away to engage in a serious war against darkness and in the morning it rises to save humankind.
10/22/11 23:51:23: UNkosiyazi: the night when evil hunts evil.

10/22/11 23:54:15: UNkosiyazi: what if i die tonight?
10/23/11 6:20:06: UNkosiyazi: gimme an opinion on Polygamy and Polyandry!

DARKIE

11/23/11 12:15:44: Darkie: I don't know hey

11/23/11 12:16:07: Darkie: Its a tough one

11/23/11 12:19:00: Darkie: I find it difficult to look back- it was so long ago we were together- what its like 6 years- u can't expect us to be on the same level- and now u r in New York- u got ur life there- u there - me here in SA

11/23/11 12:29:16: UNkosiyazi: it still doesn't excuse our manner of communication.

11/23/11 12:37:51: Darkie: Have u listened - to "Her Heart" Anthony Hamilton

11/23/11 12:42:24: UNkosiyazi: no, will do so now.

11/23/11 12:44:36: Darkie: Heee heee

11/23/11 12:55:02: Darkie: Tell me what u think after listening

11/23/11 13:02:27: UNkosiyazi: "...her love wont let me lose her no matter how i try, i just can't say goodbye and lose her."

11/23/11 13:50:26: Darkie: Uhm

11/23/11 13:50:32: Darkie: U got the song alright

11/23/11 13:51:35: Darkie: That it is how. It was supposed to be initially

11/23/11 13:59:05: UNkosiyazi: true

11/23/11 15:16:24: UNkosiyazi: <media omitted>

11/23/11 23:20:48: UNkosiyazi: <media omitted>

11/23/11 23:21:00: UNkosiyazi: Thanksgiving

11/24/11 21:20:27: UNkosiyazi: bottle after bottle till i get messed up.

11/24/11 21:57:21: UNkosiyazi: tell me, what's that song about Tkzee "ela ngwana wa ka..."?

11/26/11 1:24:59: UNkosiyazi: good morning!

11/26/11 2:26:22: UNkosiyazi: i kno we hardly say words (talk) to each other but it was sweet talkin to you.
11/26/11 3:00:00: UNkosiyazi: love without limit

11/26/11 3:00:35: Darkie: Heee heee

11/26/11 3:01:04: UNkosiyazi: truth

11/27/11 1:39:16: UNkosiyazi: how did you sleep?

11/27/11 1:41:06: Darkie: Very well thanks - and u?v

11/27/11 1:43:23: UNkosiyazi: im still up, cooking.

11/28/11 0:23:54: UNkosiyazi: goodmorning!
11/29/11 0:41:36: UNkosiyazi: hope you slept well.

11/29/11 0:43:45: Darkie: Morning

11/29/11 0:44:10: Darkie: I was watching- "The Resident"

11/29/11 0:44:34: Darkie: It had my heart beating too fast-

11/29/11 0:45:04: Darkie: So it took me a while to gather my thoughts
and sleep peacefully

11/29/11 0:49:32: UNkosiyazi: what is The Resident?

11/29/11 1:03:13: UNkosiyazi: "i just cant believe that you've been
sent to me from above. you're my angel of love. i cant wait to feel
your sunshine..."
11/29/11 1:12:46: Darkie: The Resident- is a movie

11/29/11 1:13:19: Darkie: Nope- the song does not ring a bell-
probably when I hear it

11/29/11 1:18:02: UNkosiyazi: im listenin to it while sippin Southern
Comfort...

11/29/11 1:18:12: UNkosiyazi: <media omitted>

11/29/11 14:44:45: UNkosiyazi:
http://www.realtor.com/blogs/2011/11/23/bruce-willis-lists-idaho-
home-photos/

11/29/11 15:53:38: UNkosiyazi: send me a picture or two, just wanna
see you.

11/29/11 16:41:21: UNkosiyazi: <media omitted>

11/29/11 16:41:25: UNkosiyazi: detoxing...

11/29/11 21:03:00: Darkie: <media omitted>

11/29/11 21:04:51: UNkosiyazi: oh boy!

11/29/11 21:05:26: Darkie: <media omitted>

11/29/11 21:05:51: Darkie: Gained some weight

11/29/11 21:08:36: Darkie: After the year end function

11/29/11 21:08:36: Darkie: <media omitted>

11/29/11 21:54:36: UNkosiyazi: that is not you Pumie, right?

11/29/11 21:54:53: UNkosiyazi: you just gave me an erection.

11/29/11 22:25:03: UNkosiyazi: remember: what was up with that guy that was talkin nonsense at that FanPark when we were watchin soccer in Newtown?

11/29/11 22:31:57: UNkosiyazi: just thinkin, maybe it's the Heineken, i dont know but this i kno:
11/30/11 16:05:31: UNkosiyazi: Classic material indeed...
http://yourblackwoman.blogspot.com/2011/12/meet-sara-bartman-original-video-vixen.html#more

12/1/11 15:15:41: UNkosiyazi: A spiritually evolved woman understands the difference between chasing men and choosing a husband. The difference has a profound effect on the quality of life for her, her offspring and her community. Strong married couples build wealthy families which, in turn, build affluent communities. When the majority of babies are born to single individuals, or into marriages that don‚Äôt last, you can‚Äôt sustain an economically sound community. There is a lack of physical comfort because we are not pooling resources. People are fighting over child support and stretching one income among several households.

12/2/11 1:26:22: UNkosiyazi: how did you sleep?

12/2/11 15:11:53: UNkosiyazi: <media omitted>

12/2/11 15:46:35: UNkosiyazi: <media omitted>

12/3/11 0:04:44: UNkosiyazi: mornin! is it a gud one or what?
12/3/11 15:35:00: UNkosiyazi: Lay down here beside me and we'll
cruise the caravan
12/3/11 22:17:53: Darkie: Hey lindzz

12/3/11 22:18:34: UNkosiyazi: Sthandwa sam'!

12/3/11 22:19:08: Darkie: Am sooo sleepy

12/3/11 22:19:27: Darkie: How r u?

12/3/11 22:20:58: UNkosiyazi: hahaha...
12/3/11 22:21:28: Darkie: Oh! I c

12/3/11 22:21:52: UNkosiyazi: im almost in.

12/3/11 22:23:54: Darkie: In where?

12/3/11 22:24:19: Darkie: Your dreams?

12/3/11 22:28:23: UNkosiyazi: hah! im about to get in the game. watch
the space.

12/3/11 22:36:07: Darkie: I'm watching and cheering u on

12/3/11 22:42:12: UNkosiyazi: please do, you know i used to dream
about this back when we use to chill around Wits and stuff.
12/3/11 22:51:03: UNkosiyazi: why a sad face?

12/3/11 22:52:04: Darkie: It a smily face-

12/3/11 22:55:28: UNkosiyazi: cool...

12/3/11 22:57:23: Darkie: About?

12/3/11 22:58:49: UNkosiyazi: you know what i mean!

12/3/11 23:00:27: Darkie: I do- in some way

12/3/11 23:02:19: UNkosiyazi: good.
12/3/11 23:04:27: Darkie: Ah ah- linda!

12/3/11 23:07:44: UNkosiyazi: yes, it's the truth.

12/3/11 23:47:53: UNkosiyazi: im still waiting for you to come back
to love.
12/4/11 12:53:55: UNkosiyazi: <media omitted>

12/4/11 12:53:56: UNkosiyazi: howaz yo day?
12/4/11 13:09:41: UNkosiyazi: <media omitted>

12/4/11 15:59:34: UNkosiyazi: sweet dreams.
12/4/11 18:19:14: UNkosiyazi: my snuff supply is getting depleted,
can you mail me some more?

12/5/11 12:14:18: UNkosiyazi: my snuff supply is getting depleted,
can you mail me some more?

12/5/11 12:18:30: UNkosiyazi: As in the stuff in the blue and yellow
container?

12/5/11 12:18:45: Darkie: Hey Lindz

12/5/11 12:19:05: Darkie: Hawu- u know I don't believe in those stuff

12/5/11 12:19:57: Darkie: I am christian- and those practices are not
in line with my life in Christ- who is the Lord of my Life

12/5/11 12:20:48: Darkie: The bible says we ought not to worship the dead

12/5/11 12:22:15: UNkosiyazi: but it is like buying cigarette or alcohol for your brother. your brother. im sure Christ will support feeding or clothing your brother.

12/5/11 12:29:42: Darkie: But u don't smoke it- u do rituals with it

12/5/11 12:33:06: UNkosiyazi: it doesnot matter what the street kid does with the money you give to him, whether it goes to glue or food, it is not your concern. your concern is as Jesus taught you- you give begrudgingly.

12/5/11 12:35:13: UNkosiyazi: i use it to talk to my grandmothers when i leave the house or wherever i am. it's like a rosary or thusby that reminds me to pray (talk) to my caregivers (ancestors).
12/5/11 12:37:16: UNkosiyazi: remember, even when you drink your fav beverages to spill some for them too.
12/5/11 12:49:01: UNkosiyazi: listen and learn, you gonna be a mother and a wife someday, hopefully. you gonna be a granny, God willing. you definately gonna be an ancestor, you dont have a choice.

12/6/11 23:24:07: UNkosiyazi: i like this Luther song:
Wednesday, December 7, 2011
12/7/11 11:18:30: UNkosiyazi: seems like it is going to be a good show for the Emerging Black Middle Class on SABC1:
12/7/11 12:21:55: UNkosiyazi: Philadelphia D.A. Drops Death Penalty Against Mumia Abu-Jamal
12/7/11 12:30:39: UNkosiyazi: FREE MUMIA!
12/7/11 20:20:47: UNkosiyazi: <media omitted>

12/7/11 20:31:07: UNkosiyazi: i did a film about President Zuma before he came into power, and i have never showed it to anyone. im wondering if time is right for me to release it now or should i wait until end of next year?

12/7/11 22:59:29: Darkie: It will look like a consplracy

12/7/11 23:00:37: Darkie: Especially with the upcoming ANC conference, Julias Malema suspension...

12/7/11 23:02:18: UNkosiyazi: in 2008 i said i'll realease before elections, in April of 2009 i said i'll release a year after he came into power, and now im not sure.

12/7/11 23:03:41: Darkie: Look at the climate...

12/7/11 23:04:22: Darkie: It will be banned before it even makes it to the shores

12/7/11 23:05:21: UNkosiyazi: hahaha... that i kno, my Professor at Wits in '08 said so too.

12/7/11 23:05:58: UNkosiyazi: ...but why should i fear?

12/7/11 23:06:44: Darkie: Don't, if u r up for the controversy, then go for it

12/7/11 23:07:44: Darkie: Tge thing os there is a time for everything, make sure that this is the time before u release

12/7/11 23:08:19: Darkie: Or it may be a bit premature or too late, or even better- the most favourable

12/7/11 23:09:01: Darkie: Judge that by what u want to achieve with the film, what is ur aim anyways?

12/7/11 23:10:21: UNkosiyazi: true, timing is key.
12/7/11 23:12:22: UNkosiyazi: i started reading this book about King Shaka's Aunt, Mkabayi and how she and others dealt with power and leadership- from Jama to Senzangakhona to Shaka to Dingana.

12/7/11 23:59:09: UNkosiyazi: <media omitted>

12/7/11 23:59:18: UNkosiyazi: a teaser... hah!

12/8/11 0:12:35: UNkosiyazi: <media omitted>

12/8/11 0:25:26: UNkosiyazi: <media omitted>

12/8/11 0:42:15: Darkie: I am driving - will look and comment once I get to work

12/8/11 0:42:46: UNkosiyazi: cool

12/8/11 1:55:59: UNkosiyazi: ps: the Children's Book is ready, for now it is just art (drawings) with date stamps and titles.
12/8/11 2:00:18: UNkosiyazi: ...you should get a copy for your young cousins (nieces and nephews).

12/8/11 2:25:38: UNkosiyazi: some dreams stay dreams and others dreams come true.

12/8/11 2:28:23: UNkosiyazi: Liquid Deep says: "...never let go of your dreams. no matter how hard it may seem."
12/9/11 7:39:51: Darkie: Are u far from vegas?

12/9/11 7:40:31: Darkie: Am considering going to vegas than to go to new york or chicago

12/9/11 7:41:00: Darkie: For work purposes

12/9/11 7:41:22: Darkie: Do u think its a good option?

12/9/11 9:40:40: UNkosiyazi: with Deloitte or with another firm?

12/9/11 9:41:13: UNkosiyazi: yeah, im far from Vegas.

12/9/11 9:48:55: Darkie: Deloitte

12/9/11 9:53:47: UNkosiyazi: Vegas, NY and Chi-town, seems
interesting.
12/9/11 10:11:00: Darkie: How far r u? How many minutes

12/9/11 10:11:11: Darkie: Away from NY

12/9/11 10:12:30: UNkosiyazi: couple of hours...

12/9/11 10:13:00: Darkie: how many hours?

12/9/11 10:13:10: UNkosiyazi: Five

12/9/11 10:16:03: UNkosiyazi: how much time are you spending in each
city?

12/9/11 10:16:36: Darkie: 4 months

12/9/11 10:16:58: Darkie: But I have to choose 1 city

12/9/11 10:18:10: UNkosiyazi: which time of the month you thinking of
travelling?

12/9/11 10:21:56: UNkosiyazi: NY and Chicago are exciting between May
and September and Vegas is good almost all year round- weatherwise.
Vegas is a desert and nuttin much to do but gamble.
12/10/11 0:43:58: UNkosiyazi: <media omitted>

12/10/11 0:44:00: UNkosiyazi: gudmornin!

12/10/11 0:47:47: Darkie: Yum Oreos!

12/10/11 0:48:14: Darkie: What is that- is there milk or is a big
packet of oreos

12/10/11 2:33:37: UNkosiyazi: big packet of Obams...

12/10/11 2:45:28: Darkie: ?

12/10/11 2:51:01: UNkosiyazi: Oreo = Obama = Coconut

12/10/11 2:52:30: UNkosiyazi: hah!

12/10/11 12:51:57: UNkosiyazi: AmaPantsula Ajabulile = Professor ft Kabelo
12/10/11 12:59:28: UNkosiyazi: you like Ungazoba Serious = Big NUZ?

12/10/11 14:43:45: Darkie: Unfortunately I don't know the songs-

12/10/11 14:43:47: Darkie: Probably when I hear it - I will remember

12/10/11 14:56:49: UNkosiyazi: probably

12/11/11 13:18:10: UNkosiyazi: <media omitted>

12/11/11 14:59:06: UNkosiyazi: ulale kahle

12/11/11 17:13:41: UNkosiyazi: <media omitted>

12/12/11 1:10:23: UNkosiyazi: how did you sleep?
12/12/11 2:31:59: Darkie: Morning...

12/12/11 2:31:59: Darkie: My client is based in Mpumalanga... So had to drive for 3 hours... Have just arrived

12/12/11 2:32:00: Darkie: I have been driving since 6am...

12/12/11 9:27:15: UNkosiyazi: that is gud to know, ive jus got up too. thankful for another new day to learn or do something new.

12/12/11 9:27:59: Darkie: Happy day then

12/12/11 9:28:34: Darkie: What r u going to get up to? Whilst some of us are sleeping

12/12/11 9:28:49: UNkosiyazi: oh thank u...
12/12/11 9:29:29: UNkosiyazi: just gotta go joggin and then do some reading and writing.

12/12/11 10:07:09: UNkosiyazi: time's a wastin!
12/12/11 10:11:04: UNkosiyazi: Erykah Badu:
12/12/11 10:12:56: UNkosiyazi: ...it inspires me this Badu track...

12/12/11 10:53:40: UNkosiyazi: in my dream last night, a woman was teaching me some deep doctrine and showing me some signs: i dont really recollect it all but i believe it was a sign of things to come that i will learn.
12/12/11 13:54:47: UNkosiyazi: Meet Sara Bartman: The Original Video Vixen
12/13/11 0:49:32: UNkosiyazi: it's nights like these that makes me desire you Darkie. it's full moon and minus five degrees outside.

12/13/11 15:09:53: UNkosiyazi: before you lay yourself down to sleep tonight, know that i love you and wish you well.

12/13/11 22:54:17: UNkosiyazi: "To just spend all my time
12/14/11 3:28:06: UNkosiyazi: <media omitted>

12/14/11 3:28:10: UNkosiyazi: five Corona's, im feeling nice.

12/14/11 3:48:55: UNkosiyazi: anyway, im excited coz i re-started (resumed) my Zulu novel today.

12/14/11 3:55:46: Darkie: Halala!

12/14/11 3:56:45: UNkosiyazi: work hard play hard.

12/14/11 3:57:20: UNkosiyazi: <media omitted>

12/14/11 3:57:21: UNkosiyazi: ...just twisted a bottle of Heineken.

12/14/11 3:58:10: UNkosiyazi: ...should have about 150 pages by the end of this year. im a workaholic.

12/14/11 3:59:47: UNkosiyazi: im doing seven pages per day. i will leave a mark on this planet earth.

12/14/11 4:15:57: UNkosiyazi: <media omitted>

12/14/11 4:26:12: Darkie: Hmmmm

12/14/11 4:26:24: Darkie: Ur hair brother!

12/14/11 4:27:21: Darkie: Hmmm those lips- they appear nourished and soft- yumm

12/14/11 4:29:57: UNkosiyazi: oh stop it baby. what's wrong with my hair?

12/14/11 5:04:06: UNkosiyazi: what am i trying to prove? it's five in the morning, im off to sleep.

12/14/11 14:49:38: UNkosiyazi: <media omitted>

12/17/11 22:04:12: UNkosiyazi: <media omitted>

12/19/11 1:21:23: UNkosiyazi: ...dont tell me you are still sleepin! rise and shine, it's a new day. enjoy it.
12/19/11 1:43:56: UNkosiyazi: im just watchin a program on CNN about marriage. they say in 1960 marriages were at 80% and last year they were at 41%. people prefer to co-habit now because the institution of marriage has been reduced to money, commodity and liability. evri one is pushing for a career before family. men prefer to marry one another these days.
12/19/11 1:46:06: UNkosiyazi: ive concluded that for me, im just gonna find someone who just wanna put family before career. there

turn to be unnecessary competition when both r pushing career coz
family (children) get compromised under the guise of "children are
expensive".

12/19/11 2:22:58: Darkie: You figure?

12/19/11 2:26:31: UNkosiyazi: yeah!

12/19/11 2:26:36: UNkosiyazi: ps: the CNN guy is crying over the fact
that Kobe Bryant's wife is gonna part with half of Kobe's millions,
joint custody of the children and alimony.
12/19/11 2:28:42: Darkie: But that's what bantu people r doing now

12/19/11 2:29:18: Darkie: Rather don't get married in community of
property then

12/19/11 2:30:06: UNkosiyazi: i blame the White men with his messed
up values under the disguise of church (religion).

12/19/11 2:31:07: UNkosiyazi: traditional marriage is the way to
protect the interests of the children.

12/19/11 2:47:52: UNkosiyazi: what does she want to do with my
property? my brothers are the ones to look after my property when im
gone, not umfazi. they look after my property and children until my
male children are grown ukuvusa umuzi wami (uyise wabo).
12/19/11 22:37:19: UNkosiyazi: im still feelin this Drake track:
12/19/11 22:38:01: UNkosiyazi: Patience is a Virtue that is only
possessed by a few.

12/19/11 23:11:24: UNkosiyazi: i feel creative juices tonight so
lemme share a piece i've just thought about:
12/19/11 23:31:31: Darkie: Wow- that is quite a mouthful

12/20/11 0:46:34: UNkosiyazi: thank you

12/20/11 13:21:18: UNkosiyazi: <media omitted>

12/20/11 14:43:15: UNkosiyazi: before i forget and get caught up, lemme say: enjoy your festive season (in Zulu it's called Ishwama / feast of the first fruits or harvest)!

12/21/11 4:00:37: UNkosiyazi: <media omitted>

12/21/11 20:08:56: UNkosiyazi: <media omitted>

12/21/11 23:42:16: UNkosiyazi: <media omitted>

12/22/11 0:10:17: UNkosiyazi: i love sleeping on the floor...

12/23/11 1:18:05: UNkosiyazi: here is the link to children art book by my kids: http://www.amazon.com/gp/aw/d/B006P16D1I/ref=redir_mdp_mobile
12/23/11 1:56:40: UNkosiyazi: the book is titled: CHICKENS AND GOATS

12/23/11 2:04:15: UNkosiyazi: please support it, rate it and jot a review while at it... much appreciated.
12/23/11 2:59:58: UNkosiyazi: AS I LAY ME DOWN TO SLEEP, WORDS FROM YASIIN BEY (AN ARTIST FORMERLY KNOWN AS MOS DEF) RINGS IN MY EARS WHEN HE SAYS:
12/23/11 9:25:14: UNkosiyazi: i had a gud sleep... woke up thinking:
12/23/11 10:18:19: UNkosiyazi: <media omitted>

12/23/11 10:18:24: UNkosiyazi: make time to read this. his company owns LVMH (Louis Vutton, Hennessy, Moet), Cartier, Alfred Dunhill, etc...
12/24/11 1:07:46: UNkosiyazi: <media omitted>

12/24/11 1:33:01: UNkosiyazi: Kanye West: "...50 told me go 'head switch the style up
12/24/11 1:34:44: UNkosiyazi: Rick Ross: ambition is priceless, it's in my vein.

12/24/11 2:21:30: Darkie: From 200 dollars- what can u get worth that money that side?

12/24/11 2:22:10: Darkie: There is a man who sent 200 dollars to his son for maintenance

12/24/11 2:22:12: UNkosiyazi: a lot...

12/24/11 2:22:47: Darkie: Rent? Food? Grocery for a month?

12/24/11 2:23:25: Darkie: Do u think it is enough as maintenance for ur kids?

12/24/11 2:23:53: Darkie: We r finding it unfair

12/24/11 2:24:39: Darkie: The whole year he did not support- and now is only contributing 200 dollars

12/24/11 2:25:23: UNkosiyazi: why would a child need to pay rent? a child is not a liability or a commodity. a 50 dollar grocery can last that child a month.

12/24/11 2:26:23: Darkie: Oh really

12/24/11 2:26:59: Darkie: But men need to be considerate to the mother of the kids

12/24/11 2:28:01: Darkie: The man is a doctor there in the US- never helped the mother for 3 years and now is only sending 200 dollars after 3 years

12/24/11 2:28:11: UNkosiyazi: the woman should just give the man his children so that he can raise them in the ways of his forefathers.

12/24/11 2:28:40: Darkie: He does not want the child.

12/24/11 2:29:32: Darkie: He left for the US saying they would follow him or he would return and now it is 6 years later

12/24/11 2:29:43: UNkosiyazi: maybe the mother was acting "foolish" towards the man. using the child to fight or get even with the man.

12/24/11 2:30:53: UNkosiyazi: ...im lost, thought everybody was in America.

12/24/11 2:33:28: Darkie: No she is here in SA, The ex husband is in America- they are both from Nigeria

12/24/11 2:34:52: UNkosiyazi: im sure the man has parents or grandparents, his children need to be with them not the woman.

12/24/11 2:35:11: Darkie: He studied his PHD in SA- Brought his wife and child to SA- left the wife and child in SA (since they could not get a VISA) and carrierd on to the US- to never return - till today

12/24/11 2:35:46: Darkie: The fathers family don't care about the woman and child

12/24/11 2:35:55: Darkie: Have never called

12/24/11 2:36:29: UNkosiyazi: who is saying this, the man or the "bitter" woman?

12/24/11 2:37:07: Darkie: The woman

12/24/11 2:37:16: UNkosiyazi: go figure!

12/24/11 2:38:35: UNkosiyazi: the children need to be where their father is.

12/24/11 2:40:29: UNkosiyazi: izingane ezendoda. we dont want children that grow up with complexies because their mother wouldnt listen, edaza inkani futhi eqophisana nendoda.

12/24/11 2:41:40: Darkie: Linda

12/24/11 2:42:05: Darkie: U r such a man

12/24/11 2:42:52: Darkie: Were u not raised by ur mother?

12/24/11 2:44:22: UNkosiyazi: yes, i was. my mother was cultured.

12/24/11 2:46:46: UNkosiyazi: my granny instilled order. granny was a disciplinarian, jealous down. it is why i cant take nonsense, especially from women.

12/24/11 2:48:24: Darkie: So why do u feel so strongly about men raising kids by themselves

12/24/11 2:48:45: Darkie: Leave to women ooo- they were born for this

12/24/11 2:53:26: UNkosiyazi: i didnt say a man raises children by himself. children need to be with their father. the children dont belong to the woman nor the man but to the man's ancestors.
12/24/11 2:53:50: UNkosiyazi: it takes a girl to save a nation!

12/24/11 3:02:53: UNkosiyazi: anyway, we cant reach you, you are old. our hope is to teach them while they are young.
12/24/11 10:51:27: UNkosiyazi: <media omitted>

12/24/11 10:51:48: UNkosiyazi: you like my smoothie?

12/24/11 12:39:00: UNkosiyazi: <media omitted>

12/24/11 12:39:05: UNkosiyazi: what are you reading these days?

MNTWANA

10/17/11 1:02:16: UNkosiyazi: Thuto Ke Senotlolo: Mahlathini &Mahotella Queens

10/17/11 1:03:24: UNkosiyazi: i see you, in a lonely place
10/17/11 1:03:45: UNkosiyazi: there are times, when you'll need someone
10/17/11 4:49:04: Mntwana: Lyrics 4rm?

10/17/11 7:02:12: UNkosiyazi: do your research

10/17/11 8:51:45: Mntwana: Shup, google it is..

10/17/11 9:12:49: Mntwana: Bobby Caldwell?

10/17/11 12:09:41: UNkosiyazi: is that what it says?

10/17/11 12:14:27: Mntwana: Yep, also shows some Dwele dude..

10/17/11 13:15:54: UNkosiyazi: hahaha...
10/17/11 13:17:04: UNkosiyazi: when u graduate r u gonna be an Accountant / Economist?

10/17/11 13:20:17: Mntwana: An initiative to respond to a "research project" hey..
10/17/11 13:21:14: UNkosiyazi: cool

10/17/11 13:24:46: UNkosiyazi: Germany (Jews) Reopens Nazi Cases.
10/17/11 13:25:35: Mntwana: Why reopen them?

10/17/11 13:26:12: UNkosiyazi: justice

10/17/11 13:27:13: UNkosiyazi: the blood of the dead cries from the ground for justice.
10/17/11 13:28:14: Mntwana: I dnt see that happening practically in sa..

10/17/11 13:31:34: UNkosiyazi: just you wait, in due tym.
10/17/11 13:33:09: UNkosiyazi: look how long it is taking Jews.
10/17/11 13:34:51: Mntwana: And where does "pardon/forgiveness" come in?

10/17/11 13:37:01: UNkosiyazi: not when it comes to killing.
10/17/11 13:41:04: UNkosiyazi: allow me to school you briefly: the spirit of a murdered one cannot reunite with spirit of its ancestors unless justice (retribution / revenge) is done to pacify it.
10/17/11 13:45:42: Mntwana: 'Kids' these days have no care in the world about the blood of their ancestors and demanding justice in that regard, its all about "self"..
10/17/11 13:52:19: UNkosiyazi: we'll come to them as spirits through dreams, visions and appearances.
10/17/11 13:54:33: UNkosiyazi: war and peace is like love and hate: same thing.
10/17/11 13:58:55: UNkosiyazi: a debt to collect.
10/17/11 14:03:27: Mntwana: #Peace in the midst of war is peace for some and nt 4 all..
10/17/11 14:05:27: UNkosiyazi: watch for ye know not the time when the thief will come and rob your house.

10/17/11 17:47:15: UNkosiyazi: ANCIENT BANTU HISTORY: the Zulu Surgeons of 17th century and beyond: did things that the White men hasn't even dreamt of yet.

10/17/11 21:08:05: UNkosiyazi: space and time are one and the same thing.
10/17/11 21:38:52: UNkosiyazi: where in the Bible do they get this maths: Preacher man takes ten percent of gross, government comes and

take its taxes, bills come and take almost everything. what am i left
with?
10/17/11 22:45:27: Mntwana: Do u really want me to answer that?

10/17/11 22:46:02: Mntwana: Lol "maths"

10/18/11 1:41:36: UNkosiyazi: if u want

10/18/11 2:29:21: Mntwana: Tithing is a biblical principle, a
debatable one thereof..coz it's found in the old testament and nt in
the new..
10/18/11 2:37:40: UNkosiyazi: tithes rob the poor, they dont feed the
needy nor the gods.

10/18/11 2:44:28: UNkosiyazi: on a lighter note: been dreaming about
the new "two door" Range Rover.

10/18/11 2:44:39: Mntwana: U tithe 4rm wat u have, nt wat u dnt
have..feeding the needy is a seperate responsibility that the church
has, whether they do it or nt is another story...tithing was never
mean to rob anyone and if it does, then someone is abusing the well-
being of the principle..and making it a bad thing wen it was never
meant to be bad

10/18/11 2:53:21: UNkosiyazi: what people worship nowadays is nothing
but a "social order" i tell u. has nuttin to do with God, gods (high
and low), and ancestors.
10/18/11 3:05:24: Mntwana: Dnt wana get into a debate about the dead
coz my undastanding there is limited..as u have already pointed owt..
10/18/11 3:06:20: UNkosiyazi: hahaha...

10/18/11 3:13:05: UNkosiyazi: come home Mntwana so you can understand
the deep dictrine of our great ancestors and not the rubbish the
foreigners rammed down our throats.
10/18/11 3:27:11: Mntwana: Lol..i dnt know how to respond to that..

10/18/11 3:29:18: UNkosiyazi: dont even respond, im just being an airhead and insulting. it's time i shut eyes.

10/18/11 3:37:12: Mntwana: yes, ur insulting..
10/18/11 9:14:50: UNkosiyazi: Mntwana: unjani?
10/18/11 9:51:34: Mntwana: Glad u slept well..im well hey,had a dramatic morning..lol..

10/18/11 9:59:05: UNkosiyazi: tell me about it.

10/18/11 10:46:25: Mntwana: Lady who cleans on my floor has been a problem..nt only 4 me, bt 4 half the floor..i cant stand dirty showers and wen i saw wat they lukd like yday, i had a fit..
10/18/11 10:51:12: Mntwana: Apparently they're also tired of her tendencies, so they undertook a "raid" today, inspecting all the rooms and checking on her job..
10/18/11 10:57:01: Mntwana: An nw she cums to me asking 4 sympathy whilst bad-mouthing everyone..
10/18/11 11:02:57: Mntwana: Res politics...and i just had to be in the middle of it all..

10/18/11 12:24:12: UNkosiyazi: interesting

10/18/11 13:15:23: Mntwana: Abanye abantu bayavilapha..if they dnt wana do their job, then im here, il make sure they do it

10/18/11 13:18:44: UNkosiyazi: gudluck...
10/18/11 13:20:33: Mntwana: Of course, all respect is due there..they mustn't take advantage of that fact tho

10/20/11 8:43:44: UNkosiyazi: Young Girls and the Dangers of the 'Booty Pose'.
10/20/11 10:06:06: Mntwana: Wat dangers are these?

10/20/11 12:16:36: UNkosiyazi: "booty pose"

10/20/11 12:27:28: UNkosiyazi:
http://yourblackwoman.blogspot.com/2011/10/sojourner-marable-
grimmett-young-girls.html

10/20/11 12:52:53: Mntwana: ....really didn't see this as
posing a significant threat.
10/20/11 12:57:08: UNkosiyazi: it's a big problem.
10/20/11 13:03:00: Mntwana: Bad influence even to us 'young ladies'
10/20/11 13:05:31: UNkosiyazi: stay awake

10/21/11 11:34:53: Mntwana: <media omitted>

10/21/11 11:35:11: Mntwana: My frens and i..at a get-together

10/21/11 13:17:41: Mntwana: <media omitted>

10/21/11 13:17:42: Mntwana: Wen we play, we play..

10/21/11 13:19:15: Mntwana: <media omitted>

10/21/11 13:19:29: Mntwana: Ghetto style:)

10/21/11 17:38:40: Mntwana: FB.Status of a frend-
10/21/11 18:37:07: UNkosiyazi: unjani?

10/21/11 18:37:52: UNkosiyazi: <media omitted>

10/21/11 18:40:03: Mntwana: Except 4 being tired, id like to think im
gud..
10/21/11 18:41:02: UNkosiyazi: tired, sick and stuff.

10/21/11 18:42:19: UNkosiyazi: had a terrible running stomach da
whole of last nite and had to be on film set da whole day today. was
shittin on words.

10/21/11 18:48:14: Mntwana: Still nt well?

10/21/11 18:48:37: Mntwana: Hw u feeling nw?

10/21/11 19:16:04: UNkosiyazi: still sick, im just indoors taking it easy tryna conserve energy for work tomorrow.

10/21/11 19:16:10: UNkosiyazi: in 2008 in South Africa: 54% Whites graduated with PhD's while Blacks were 13%. what a shame- we need KNOWLEDGE CREATORS. let us pursue high education &encourage others. Whites are going to rule and control us if we are not careful. our children should know from word go that the lowest level of education for them is PhD.

10/21/11 19:21:24: Mntwana: Hope u feel beta soon..
10/21/11 19:23:07: Mntwana: Sleepy..im crashing 4rm a caffeine high..

10/21/11 19:26:50: UNkosiyazi: gudnite

10/21/11 19:27:00: UNkosiyazi: food for thought:

10/21/11 19:27:04: UNkosiyazi: come now!
10/21/11 19:29:40: Mntwana: Feel like i just read a riddle..

10/21/11 19:34:29: UNkosiyazi: like i said: "food for thought".
10/22/11 18:47:20: UNkosiyazi: feel so much betta than ngoLwesine kanye nangoLwesihlanu.

10/22/11 23:47:22: UNkosiyazi: the sun goes away to engage in a serious war against darkness and in the morning it rises to save humankind.
10/22/11 23:47:39: UNkosiyazi: ungrateful

10/22/11 23:50:59: UNkosiyazi: the night when evil hunts evil.

10/22/11 23:53:39: UNkosiyazi: what if i die tonight?
http://www.nytimes.com/2011/10/23/technology/at-waldorf-school-in-silicon-valley-technology-can-wait.html?pagewanted=all

10/23/11 1:04:32: Mntwana: Glad ur feeling beta

10/23/11 4:01:57: Mntwana: Those last two msgs..dnt know wat u going
on about

10/23/11 5:09:28: UNkosiyazi: hahaha...
10/23/11 5:12:55: Mntwana: Alryti.. ur up early..

10/23/11 5:13:59: UNkosiyazi: ...gotta be on film set in two hours.

10/23/11 5:22:15: Mntwana: Oh i see, u had the same thing going on
yday?

10/23/11 5:32:00: UNkosiyazi: since Friday.

10/23/11 5:32:13: UNkosiyazi: <media omitted>

10/23/11 5:42:46: UNkosiyazi: that clip is from a film im working on.

10/23/11 5:47:18: Mntwana: Always takes me a while to download ur
videos, coz i cnt watch them 4rm my fone

10/23/11 5:51:15: UNkosiyazi: ooops

10/23/11 5:52:20: Mntwana: It's kul...
10/23/11 5:53:32: UNkosiyazi: ...dont know about that, it is supposed
to be in realtime.

10/23/11 5:55:23: Mntwana: Oh no, i mean are the guys still
rehearsing?

10/23/11 5:55:38: Mntwana: Wats the film about

10/23/11 5:58:10: UNkosiyazi: yeah, still rehearsing.
10/23/11 6:05:48: Mntwana: Ayt, the only time i undastand "action"
sorta movies, is if someone xplains them to me..

10/23/11 6:07:02: UNkosiyazi: funny

10/23/11 6:07:07: UNkosiyazi: by da way, the guy that is throwing foliage is Dave Chappelle's step-brother. he is the one who choreographed the fighting scene.

10/23/11 6:12:00: Mntwana: Guess il have to google this Dave Chappelle..

10/23/11 6:16:05: UNkosiyazi: are you even asking!

10/23/11 6:18:45: Mntwana: Lol..

10/23/11 6:18:59: UNkosiyazi: gimme an opinion on Polygamy and Polyandry!

10/23/11 6:21:47: Mntwana: Lol, polyandry ne..this is gona take a while..

10/23/11 6:22:45: Mntwana: thought i gave u an opinion on polygamy tho

10/23/11 6:26:27: UNkosiyazi: an opinion polygamy in conjuction with polyandry.
10/23/11 6:30:30: Mntwana: Cnt even undastand why a woman wud wana have more than one husband..cnt get my head around it..
10/23/11 6:32:18: UNkosiyazi: interesting.
10/23/11 6:34:22: UNkosiyazi: ...what / whose surname does she take?

10/23/11 6:34:27: Mntwana: Dnt u think that all her husbands wud want kids 4rm her?
10/23/11 6:35:10: UNkosiyazi: they have to have kids.

10/23/11 6:36:50: Mntwana: Well exactly..I dnt think changing surnames wud b an option..she'd have to keep hers..

10/23/11 6:39:41: Mntwana: having a triple-barrel surname...na..unfortunately, nt everything is fair..polygamy we can live with..polyandry on the other hand makes me question 'self-respect'

10/23/11 6:40:10: UNkosiyazi: hahaha...

10/23/11 6:44:21: UNkosiyazi: if she has five consorts and they all want five kids each: means that if she starts at 20 years old she'll be birthing them for the next 25 years.
10/23/11 6:48:35: Mntwana: Uphilele ukuzala i'ingane? Kahleni bo..its nt about whether she can or nt, it's about whether her body cud take that or nt..quite frankly, she'd probarbly have a short life..id rather keep the period pains, thank u very much

10/23/11 6:53:02: UNkosiyazi: but she has five consorts of her choice, men of her dreams and she wants to give them her love. she has eggs and they have bucket loads of semen to go around.
10/23/11 6:55:59: Mntwana: And wat kinda man who stand 4 that?

10/23/11 6:57:24: Mntwana: We aint talking bwt a fling here

10/23/11 7:03:17: UNkosiyazi: funny.
10/23/11 7:05:17: UNkosiyazi: one man and one hundred women: nation can spread.
10/23/11 7:11:15: Mntwana: Well that makes sense; providing concubines..
10/23/11 7:13:23: UNkosiyazi: we can close the case?
10/23/11 7:15:00: Mntwana: Im kul thanx, gota perspire ova the books instead..
10/23/11 7:15:07: UNkosiyazi: ps: much respect for your opinions and the fact that we can conversate about such (any thing).

10/23/11 7:16:18: Mntwana: Well im glad:):):)

10/23/11 7:17:09: UNkosiyazi: anytime

10/23/11 8:37:03: UNkosiyazi: what can South Africa learn from this:
10/23/11 8:43:09: UNkosiyazi: i miss my township school.
10/23/11 9:41:57: Mntwana: I couldn't agree more..

10/23/11 18:59:00: UNkosiyazi: truth, right?

10/24/11 2:27:58: Mntwana: Yea, "technology can wait".
10/24/11 2:36:33: UNkosiyazi: same here.
10/24/11 2:46:27: Mntwana: Gudnyt:)

10/24/11 2:50:10: UNkosiyazi: i think it's going to be "goodmornin"
coz i cant fall asleep anymore.

10/24/11 2:56:23: Mntwana: Were u ever asleepi

10/24/11 2:59:50: UNkosiyazi: yeah, got home around six pm and
crashed an hour later. im fixin to get up around five am so i can
read.

10/24/11 3:01:39: UNkosiyazi: Come Live With Me Angel: Marvin Gaye

10/24/11 3:04:23: Mntwana: In that case, gudmorning then..im just
getn ready to start my day @the library..first exam nxt monday

10/24/11 3:05:07: UNkosiyazi: ...study well

10/24/11 3:12:49: UNkosiyazi: Colder Are My Nights

10/24/11 3:13:22: UNkosiyazi: ps: howiz yo sister, mother and father?

10/24/11 3:22:22: Mntwana: Thank u..
10/24/11 3:27:54: UNkosiyazi: oh, and brother. mustnt forget
granny(ies) too.
10/24/11 3:29:40: Mntwana: Lol, y a special shout-out to her

10/24/11 3:30:10: UNkosiyazi: hahaha...

10/24/11 3:30:31: UNkosiyazi: coz she has a chiskop- funny.

10/24/11 3:34:51: Mntwana: Lol, Mxm..

10/24/11 3:39:13: Mntwana: I shud consider having a haircut then..

10/24/11 3:40:45: UNkosiyazi: u funny...

10/24/11 4:41:34: Mntwana: Flip it's so hot in jhb today

10/24/11 4:47:56: UNkosiyazi: im craving for a warm December too.
10/24/11 4:49:33: Mntwana: And it's warmer there?
10/24/11 4:54:10: UNkosiyazi: hahaha... gud ol Wartenweiler.
10/24/11 4:59:11: Mntwana: Impela angazi bengingenwe yini..it's like
a playground 4 Indians to play cards and have a picnic..
10/24/11 5:02:25: UNkosiyazi: we use a quarter system not semester.
next year September we gonna start using semesters.

10/24/11 5:08:39: UNkosiyazi: lemme take a nap, got an 8am class.
10/24/11 5:09:49: Mntwana: Ayt, sleep/nap well

10/24/11 14:20:35: UNkosiyazi: <media omitted>

10/24/11 14:20:41: UNkosiyazi: ...this morning around campus.

10/24/11 14:37:49: Mntwana: The way u tend to look so serious in ur
videos, just amuses me..

10/24/11 16:23:09: UNkosiyazi: hahaha...
10/24/11 16:29:52: Mntwana: Lol, it's funny tho..
10/24/11 17:01:40: UNkosiyazi: sweet, it shuld stay that way.

10/24/11 17:01:57: UNkosiyazi: <media omitted>

10/24/11 17:02:52: Mntwana: Really nw, y

10/24/11 17:03:00: UNkosiyazi: ...guess what it is

10/24/11 17:03:31: UNkosiyazi: it's about balance.

10/24/11 17:07:17: Mntwana: Lemons? Is this a trick question

10/24/11 17:10:18: UNkosiyazi: hahaha... lemons with what?

10/24/11 17:11:36: Mntwana: Water, sugar, WINE? I dnt know

10/24/11 17:12:18: UNkosiyazi: hey, sugar.

10/24/11 17:13:23: Mntwana: An ul b doing wat with that

10/24/11 17:13:55: UNkosiyazi: im eatin it...

10/24/11 17:14:37: UNkosiyazi: ive just added ginger.

10/24/11 17:14:57: Mntwana: But why

10/24/11 17:15:43: UNkosiyazi: it's my med-lemon

10/24/11 17:18:48: Mntwana: It helps? My goodness, i can imagine the taste of that thing

10/24/11 17:23:13: UNkosiyazi: yeah, had it Friday night and it worked.
10/24/11 17:27:36: Mntwana: Alryt, i might just try it sometime

10/24/11 19:43:08: UNkosiyazi: ps: do i intimidate you?

10/24/11 19:44:01: Mntwana: Why u wana know

10/24/11 19:44:45: UNkosiyazi: inquisitive

10/24/11 19:47:12: Mntwana: Ur height does..

10/24/11 19:47:47: UNkosiyazi: i love that.

10/24/11 19:48:22: Mntwana: lol, I dnt think anything else does

10/24/11 19:48:46: UNkosiyazi: cool

10/24/11 19:49:07: Mntwana: Y u love that

10/24/11 19:50:02: UNkosiyazi: it means i have a "presence".
10/24/11 19:51:12: Mntwana: Lol, oh u do..no doubt there

10/24/11 19:58:35: UNkosiyazi: hahaha...

10/24/11 21:09:43: UNkosiyazi: what is the rate of men marrying
virgin women?

10/24/11 21:15:22: UNkosiyazi: a firstborn child born from a virgin
woman is special.

10/24/11 21:21:48: UNkosiyazi: a virgin woman (women) in a society /
community is PRICELESS.

10/24/11 21:26:48: UNkosiyazi: we need virgins in our society. please
encourage girls / ladies you know to preserve their virginity
(innocence). it is the "in-thing", it is "sexy".

10/25/11 0:43:16: Mntwana: What about virgin men?

10/25/11 7:59:19: UNkosiyazi: are you seriously going to ask me that
question given our prior discussions on polygamy and polyandry?

10/25/11 8:01:26: Mntwana: I guess i wasn't really looking 4 an
answer

10/25/11 8:01:51: UNkosiyazi: i thought so too

10/25/11 8:02:24: UNkosiyazi: unjani, anyway?

10/25/11 8:05:19: Mntwana: Very funny..lol..
10/25/11 8:26:16: UNkosiyazi: slept well, dreamt well.

10/25/11 8:26:49: UNkosiyazi: u must get umsebenzi done for u
quickly.

10/25/11 10:00:41: Mntwana: I still dnt know wat umsebenzi entails

10/25/11 12:16:34: UNkosiyazi: what wuld u loose by not asking your
elders?

10/25/11 13:06:55: UNkosiyazi: i wonder if Christianity didn't
introduce wedding of the Whites (white wedding) will my sister be so
fixated about "walking down the aisle"?

10/25/11 13:08:37: UNkosiyazi: rich and highly educated people of
India still have "fixed marriages".
10/25/11 17:52:15: UNkosiyazi: <media omitted>

10/25/11 17:52:20: UNkosiyazi: ...at the end of the day!

10/25/11 17:55:58: UNkosiyazi: <media omitted>

10/25/11 18:06:09: UNkosiyazi: <media omitted>

10/25/11 18:08:30: UNkosiyazi: trick-o-treat night

10/25/11 18:25:32: Mntwana: Too cute..

10/25/11 18:25:54: Mntwana: The kids, that isn't

10/25/11 18:26:03: Mntwana: is..

10/25/11 18:27:19: UNkosiyazi: u funny

10/25/11 18:29:58: Mntwana: No insinuations..

10/25/11 18:31:44: UNkosiyazi: none at all

10/25/11 18:51:50: Mntwana: Fixed marriages as in "arranged"?

10/25/11 18:56:01: UNkosiyazi: yes

10/26/11 1:04:00: UNkosiyazi: im tired

10/26/11 7:00:33: Mntwana: <media omitted>

10/26/11 7:00:35: Mntwana: On the roof..

10/26/11 7:37:15: UNkosiyazi: oh sweet, nice clip.
10/26/11 7:41:12: Mntwana: More like "enjoying" heat waves..
10/26/11 7:55:57: UNkosiyazi: gudmornin,
10/26/11 23:31:27: UNkosiyazi: Brown Eyed Girl: Tevin Campbell
10/27/11 2:07:12: Mntwana: Seems to rain quite often there..

10/27/11 10:14:35: UNkosiyazi: oh yeah, maybe it's the signs.

10/27/11 10:15:04: UNkosiyazi: hahaha...
10/27/11 10:20:13: Mntwana: An wats so funny

10/27/11 12:42:08: UNkosiyazi: ...the fact that we dont see the
storms coming. we are like people of Noah. he told them to put their
houses in order but abamshayanga ndiva.

10/27/11 13:36:21: Mntwana: Ayt, ayt..

10/27/11 17:15:15: Mntwana: <media omitted>

10/27/11 17:15:23: Mntwana: She gets easily distracted at the library

10/27/11 17:16:11: UNkosiyazi: why does she?

10/27/11 17:19:06: Mntwana: Anxiety..

10/27/11 17:19:42: UNkosiyazi: ...or ADD maybe?
10/27/11 17:21:30: Mntwana: Lol, il reserve my comment on that one

10/27/11 17:22:49: UNkosiyazi: Mmmm...!

10/27/11 17:29:42: UNkosiyazi: Eddie Zondi be still talkin about same ol same ol issues that don't progress.

10/27/11 17:29:58: UNkosiyazi: ...sugar mommies

10/27/11 17:38:48: Mntwana: Lol..well maybe it's what the listeners want to be talking bwt /hearing

10/27/11 17:40:50: UNkosiyazi: not at all.
10/27/11 17:44:54: Mntwana: People such as yourself?
10/27/11 17:46:25: UNkosiyazi: uyahlekisa

10/27/11 17:51:42: UNkosiyazi: itchin for a vacation

10/27/11 17:52:43: Mntwana: Nomads...#rolling eyes#

10/27/11 17:54:03: UNkosiyazi: exactly: what do you think the word "Zulu" means?

10/27/11 17:57:02: Mntwana: Im nt gona crack my skull tryna think about it
10/27/11 18:00:30: UNkosiyazi: hahaha...
10/27/11 18:01:21: UNkosiyazi: ...im kiddin.
10/27/11 18:01:44: UNkosiyazi: Xhosa's

10/27/11 18:02:26: Mntwana: Lol..il let that slide...
10/27/11 18:02:59: UNkosiyazi: i shuld start charging you for teaching you about your identity.

10/27/11 18:05:00: Mntwana: Hahahaha, i didn't grow up with other Zulu's, everything i know i learnt 4rm the parents..

10/27/11 18:08:11: UNkosiyazi: isn't that what parenting is about?

10/27/11 18:10:45: Mntwana: Well exactly...

10/27/11 18:14:54: UNkosiyazi: between me, you and Powers that Be: one day &your ancestors willing, you'll come to realise that Christianity is a lie.
10/27/11 18:17:19: Mntwana: On what basis do u say that?

10/27/11 18:17:45: UNkosiyazi: i say ol of these because if i start explaining what Zulu means you'll get confused because of what you've been taught in school and in church.
10/27/11 18:19:46: UNkosiyazi: for example: what would you say if i tell you that God does not answer your prayers but you answer your own prayers?

10/27/11 18:20:32: Mntwana: Id just ask why u say that

10/27/11 18:20:59: UNkosiyazi: exactly.
10/27/11 18:21:57: Mntwana: Huge assumption there..so because i wont undastand, i should never know?

10/27/11 18:23:37: UNkosiyazi: u hav 2 cum home first then u'll understand.
10/27/11 18:25:17: UNkosiyazi: anyway: im itchin for a vacation

10/27/11 18:26:22: UNkosiyazi: you know what the word Nguni means?

10/27/11 18:28:26: Mntwana: So u can start questioning my "zuluness" again, nna ke sharp, im nt answering that question

10/27/11 18:28:52: Mntwana: U shud scratch the itch..

10/27/11 18:30:33: UNkosiyazi: i gotta question your "Zuluness" because i want u to regain your consciousness.

10/27/11 18:31:04: UNkosiyazi: yes, REGAIN YOUR CONSCIOUSNESS.

10/27/11 18:31:21: Mntwana: At a fee?

10/27/11 18:32:00: UNkosiyazi: what if you're a Fallen Angel that i stumbled upon on my travels (journey)?

10/27/11 18:32:46: Mntwana: U must stil tel me wat u mean by fallen angel

10/27/11 18:35:33: UNkosiyazi: once u trace your ancestry line (genealogy) down to Malandela, then i'll answer u.

10/27/11 18:37:01: Mntwana: Ay bandla...

10/27/11 18:39:56: UNkosiyazi: this is serious Mntwanasenkosi: storms are coming so we need to get our houses in order.
10/27/11 18:44:42: Mntwana: Funny that u shud quote biblical instances so much..

10/27/11 18:45:48: Mntwana: I dnt doubt the seriousness, u just nt making me undastand here hence..

10/27/11 18:49:35: UNkosiyazi: hahaha...
10/27/11 18:52:17: UNkosiyazi: don't say u were never warned.
10/27/11 19:00:26: Mntwana: Never warned about "coming back home"?
10/27/11 19:04:10: UNkosiyazi: exactly my point

10/27/11 23:59:20: UNkosiyazi: time is passing by very fast, i get old everyday and i wonder if i'll ever achieve in time all that i came here on earth for.

10/28/11 3:29:01: Mntwana: The feeling is pretty mutual

10/28/11 8:44:17: UNkosiyazi: i hear u.
10/28/11 9:21:01: UNkosiyazi: Arab Slave Trade: African-Indians
(Siddis), African-Iranians, African-Arabs, African-Pakistanis, the
list goes on.
10/28/11 9:23:59: UNkosiyazi: <media omitted>

10/28/11 16:12:30: Mntwana: <media omitted>

10/28/11 16:12:45: Mntwana: Thats 18grand on me..lol

10/28/11 17:04:16: UNkosiyazi: interestin...
10/28/11 18:14:04: Mntwana: Undue connection problems, cnt seem to be
able to download anything ryt nw..

10/28/11 18:22:08: Mntwana: Whose the lady

10/28/11 18:24:28: UNkosiyazi: hahaha...
10/28/11 18:25:32: Mntwana: Why 'talk' in inverted commas

10/28/11 18:26:57: UNkosiyazi: gentleman's affair

10/28/11 19:51:47: UNkosiyazi: i'll never forget how Sir George Grey
used raw trickery on Nongqawuze that almost annihalated the Xhosa
people.
10/28/11 20:57:45: UNkosiyazi: Christianity is keeping us contained,
pacified and divided.
10/29/11 5:53:54: Mntwana: The more i ask questions, the more u just
choose nt to answer them..i cant respond to something i have no
understanding of...
10/29/11 16:12:41: UNkosiyazi: unjani?

10/29/11 16:43:58: Mntwana: U asking cause u really wana know or u
just be courteous?

10/29/11 21:11:22: UNkosiyazi: ...it's whatever.

10/30/11 1:00:33: UNkosiyazi: what kind of spell is mankind under?

10/30/11 2:18:24: Mntwana: Wats with the question

10/30/11 2:19:19: UNkosiyazi: hahaha...

10/30/11 2:22:24: Mntwana: Wats so funny

10/30/11 2:22:33: UNkosiyazi: i think i bore u.

10/30/11 2:25:30: Mntwana: No you don't, im genuinely always interested in wateva u gota say

10/30/11 2:46:48: UNkosiyazi: interestin...

10/30/11 2:51:41: Mntwana: U can be upsetting though sometimes

10/30/11 2:53:24: UNkosiyazi: <media omitted>

10/30/11 2:55:22: Mntwana: Honey? Real honey or "honey"

10/30/11 2:58:30: UNkosiyazi: u funny.
10/30/11 2:58:44: Mntwana: Nvm, got the answer

10/30/11 2:59:03: UNkosiyazi: bsides, what's the difference?

10/30/11 2:59:59: Mntwana: Lol, "honey" is the one that looks like alcohol

10/30/11 3:00:43: UNkosiyazi: hahaha... tji tji tji...

10/30/11 3:10:00: UNkosiyazi: "U can be upsetting though sometimes"
10/30/11 3:15:34: Mntwana: Act ignorant? I dnt act ignorant..wateva thats supposed to mean

10/30/11 3:17:00: UNkosiyazi: gudnight / gudmorning

10/30/11 3:18:24: Mntwana: Gudnyt

10/30/11 3:38:32: UNkosiyazi: Will i live my life chasing after women?
10/30/11 3:41:23: Mntwana: Woa...

10/30/11 20:24:12: UNkosiyazi: http://nyti.ms/ujgHRH

10/30/11 22:17:01: UNkosiyazi: The last ship, 'Umlazi 43,' arrived at Port Natal on July 21, 1911.

10/31/11 7:13:48: Mntwana: Interesting

10/31/11 13:50:03: UNkosiyazi: http://yourblackwoman.blogspot.com/2011/10/rough-cut-for-new-film-fathers-day.html

10/31/11 14:44:37: Mntwana: One of those touchy issues so many of us
10/31/11 14:47:05: Mntwana: The storms that bad?! #shocking..

10/31/11 16:51:33: UNkosiyazi: gudnyt

10/31/11 16:56:59: Mntwana: Why gudnyt?

10/31/11 17:01:33: UNkosiyazi: coz im assuming u r about to go to bed.
10/31/11 17:02:53: UNkosiyazi: im about to go play indoor ,öΩ

10/31/11 17:03:37: Mntwana: Oh no, late sleep tendencies 4 me...
10/31/11 18:45:38: UNkosiyazi: hahaha...
10/31/11 18:46:09: UNkosiyazi: ...jus got back.

10/31/11 18:47:28: Mntwana: Nice!

10/31/11 19:16:04: UNkosiyazi: nice song...
10/31/11 19:17:10: Mntwana: SWV as in?

10/31/11 19:17:35: UNkosiyazi: Sisters With Voices

10/31/11 20:00:22: UNkosiyazi: To Be Young, Gifted and Black: Donny Hathaway

10/31/11 20:05:27: UNkosiyazi: He Ain't Heavy, He's My Brother: Donny Hathaway

11/1/11 5:11:06: Mntwana: @ 11:11 11.01.11

11/1/11 3:45:48: UNkosiyazi: text me when it's 11:11 11.01.11

11/1/11 2:13:25: UNkosiyazi: gudmornin

11/1/11 2:17:18: Mntwana: Mawnin'

11/1/11 2:23:50: UNkosiyazi: to the Aztec nation: happy DIA DE LOS ANGELITOS today (Nov 1).
11/1/11 2:24:50: Mntwana: U know i cant read that language ryt?

11/1/11 2:29:53: UNkosiyazi: it's Spanish. Dia de los Angelitos (The day of Little Angels / Children) and Dia de los Muertos (The day of the Dead).
11/1/11 2:31:32: Mntwana: Oh I see..

11/1/11 2:38:27: UNkosiyazi: we live and we learn.

11/1/11 2:38:57: Mntwana: Yep

11/1/11 2:44:24: UNkosiyazi: isikhathi siyashesha.
11/1/11 2:46:42: Mntwana: Wrote one yday, 3 left..
11/1/11 2:47:37: UNkosiyazi: what was it about?

11/1/11 2:49:35: Mntwana: Twas accounting, four and a half hrs..twas just a long paper, no time to think..didn't finish my paper

11/1/11 2:53:24: UNkosiyazi: mmmhhhm...

11/1/11 2:54:22: Mntwana: Thanx 4 asking

11/1/11 2:54:53: UNkosiyazi: no sarcacism?

11/1/11 2:57:11: Mntwana: Lol...not initialy, but now that u asking..

11/1/11 2:59:25: UNkosiyazi: u r funny.

11/1/11 3:08:21: Mntwana: Lol..now u funny

11/1/11 3:09:21: UNkosiyazi: im tryna mirror yo "funnyness".
11/1/11 3:10:27: Mntwana: I feel flattered to be that role model

11/1/11 3:30:33: Mntwana: Ulale kahle mawusulala

11/1/11 3:37:34: UNkosiyazi: ngiyabonga Sthandwa sami.

11/1/11 3:46:48: Mntwana: Oh ya..alryt, hope i dont forget

11/1/11 6:12:17: Mntwana: Found some moments i captured a while ago
ekhaya that id like to share wit u...
11/1/11 6:12:56: Mntwana: <media omitted>

11/1/11 6:13:47: Mntwana: <media omitted>

11/1/11 6:14:05: Mntwana: Excuse the quality of the videos, i wasn't
using an iPhone

11/1/11 9:13:26: UNkosiyazi: Now, that's what im talking about,
families having fun and celebrating their culture.

11/1/11 9:14:25: UNkosiyazi: ...dont hate that sum of us can pick up
these bricks (iPhones) from the street.
11/1/11 9:16:09: Mntwana: Lol, one of those good things..

11/1/11 9:16:14: UNkosiyazi: <media omitted>

11/1/11 9:17:31: UNkosiyazi: love seeing Bantu people having fun.
11/1/11 9:18:28: Mntwana: Thanx, i appreciate, will do..

11/1/11 9:27:52: Mntwana: Lol, u got a charming smile

11/1/11 9:29:24: UNkosiyazi: musa ukungiqeda wena ngensini.
11/1/11 9:32:31: Mntwana: Lol, i wasn't tryna be funny, it's just fact..
11/1/11 9:36:38: UNkosiyazi: ngiyazibongela.

11/1/11 9:43:33: Mntwana: U welcome, enjoy your day

11/1/11 12:28:26: UNkosiyazi: ...dont forget to get umsebenzi done for you over the December break.

11/1/11 12:31:59: Mntwana: Family wudnt agree to having it done

11/1/11 12:35:47: UNkosiyazi: how old are you?

11/1/11 12:38:14: Mntwana: Old enuf to make my own decisions

11/1/11 12:40:25: UNkosiyazi: exactly.

11/1/11 12:41:32: UNkosiyazi: consult with them first to show them respect but as you said: u r old enuff to make your own decisions that will benefit them also.

11/1/11 12:43:44: UNkosiyazi: if u dont sort these things now, they will mess up w/your marriage life.
11/1/11 12:43:49: Mntwana: Im still gona find owt wat it entails and wat it's all about and until then, i can't say im gona have it done

11/1/11 12:47:33: UNkosiyazi: dont say u were never warned.

11/1/11 12:56:21: UNkosiyazi: go consult tomorrow when u wake up.

11/1/11 12:56:44: UNkosiyazi: u dont have to wait till things go bad.

11/1/11 13:08:54: Mntwana: Clash of beliefs..
11/1/11 13:13:12: UNkosiyazi: fair enough

11/1/11 13:13:58: Mntwana: Thanx

11/1/11 19:27:16: UNkosiyazi: "Too many drinks have been given to me
11/2/11 13:22:21: UNkosiyazi: $725 000 for a wrist watch.
11/2/11 13:33:20: Mntwana: Was discussing such things with my frends
the other day..tried making sense of it..it's ridiculous

11/2/11 15:32:58: UNkosiyazi: what do you mean "it's ridiculous"?

11/2/11 15:35:58: Mntwana: The cost is..thats just me being
analytical

11/2/11 15:39:56: UNkosiyazi: it is not ridiculous.
11/2/11 15:51:15: Mntwana: Well it's 6mil in my country dear..
11/2/11 15:59:12: UNkosiyazi: true...

11/2/11 16:00:11: UNkosiyazi: 6 million rands will be nothing to you
too when you become a partner / owner of your accounting / consulting
firm.

11/2/11 16:10:03: Mntwana: I think return on investment..that watch
may depreciate, the cost far exceeds the benefit..

11/2/11 16:11:43: Mntwana: I like that vote of confidence..here-
here:D

11/2/11 16:13:57: UNkosiyazi: hahaha...
11/2/11 16:15:07: Mntwana: Alryt, i give up the argument

11/2/11 16:16:12: Mntwana: Thanx 4 the spelling lesson

11/2/11 16:18:08: Mntwana: ...I'd probarbly have to move up to the States to sell/auction that thing..

11/2/11 16:19:08: UNkosiyazi: u funny

11/2/11 16:19:40: UNkosiyazi: ...u can always join da Billionaires Club.

11/2/11 16:20:03: UNkosiyazi: ...w/out even being inda US.

11/2/11 16:22:51: Mntwana: I Like ur thinking lol..lemme just work on getting into the "thousandaires club" first

11/2/11 16:28:57: UNkosiyazi: ...never ever think small.

11/2/11 16:32:23: Mntwana: Step-by-step..thats all i was implying..
11/2/11 16:34:16: UNkosiyazi: remember, education is not enough.
11/2/11 16:36:29: Mntwana: Nice one. Very true

11/2/11 16:40:43: UNkosiyazi: what's the point of us knowing each other if we not gonna elevate each other.

11/2/11 16:48:45: Mntwana: (",) point taken

11/2/11 19:12:22: Mntwana: Aaaah, i just saw the most biggest, super radiant star ever, so bright my mouth just dropped open..and so visible it felt like i was luking at a planet..
11/2/11 19:32:56: UNkosiyazi: hahaha...
11/2/11 19:34:58: Mntwana: Oh well, em eyes can't b bartered..
11/3/11 9:55:15: UNkosiyazi: <media omitted>

11/3/11 13:12:04: Mntwana: (~~,)

11/3/11 13:21:27: UNkosiyazi: what's the difference: in the West they marry them and divorce them, marry them and divorce them, marry them and divorce them..., they even have mistresses on the side.

11/3/11 13:25:39: Mntwana: No difrence, polygamy is a nicer way of formalizing cheating..
11/3/11 13:26:06: UNkosiyazi: ...basically, that man has lots of children from these various women. these mothers of his kids share the "same" man.
11/3/11 13:27:04: UNkosiyazi: ...wont shoot u coz man dont cheat.
11/3/11 13:30:32: Mntwana: Lol..Ukungathembeki

11/3/11 13:31:29: Mntwana: whether the word exists or not, it doesn't make it ok

11/3/11 13:32:15: Mntwana: Perhaps it be good in some way, but whats good has got to b right as well

11/3/11 13:32:54: UNkosiyazi: hahaha...

11/3/11 13:34:13: UNkosiyazi: he is called: isoka.
11/3/11 13:35:06: Mntwana: Circumcision?

11/3/11 13:35:07: UNkosiyazi: isishimane, ini?
11/3/11 13:36:11: Mntwana: I await your point

11/3/11 13:36:22: UNkosiyazi: wrong! circumcision and initiation are two different things.
11/3/11 13:37:55: Mntwana: I was close

11/3/11 13:38:34: Mntwana: especially 4 someone who is not at all xhosa, so excuse me

11/3/11 13:46:21: UNkosiyazi: Xhosa and Zulu are Nguni family.

11/3/11 13:48:16: Mntwana: I dont dispute that

11/3/11 13:58:19: UNkosiyazi: im tryna prepare you for the future and reality that awaits you so you won't go and say: men are "dogs", they are "gods". your Lord and husband whom you should support on his God given mission.

11/3/11 14:04:16: Mntwana: Lol, ay thula ntombi yase Mazizini..
11/3/11 14:05:25: UNkosiyazi: nice

11/3/11 20:30:37: UNkosiyazi: enjoyin yo sleep?

11/4/11 2:20:03: UNkosiyazi: "...this is my moment, i waited all my life. i can tell it's time"
11/4/11 2:56:55: Mntwana: Lol, i enjoyed it yes

11/4/11 3:05:00: UNkosiyazi: "i apologize i don't recollect your name. but lemme tell you that them heels really compliment your frame. girl lemme get them ooh aahs tgen i gotta catch my plane. say ya miss me and ya wishing for some private time. girl how could we get that way?"
11/4/11 3:14:41: Mntwana: Interesting coupl'a lines

11/4/11 3:17:33: UNkosiyazi: im enjoyin this track

11/4/11 3:25:46: UNkosiyazi: u like: Dance Ass?
11/4/11 3:39:49: UNkosiyazi: "...i think im addicted to naked pictures and sittin talkin bout chicks that we almost had. i dont think im conscious of making monsters outta the women that i sponsor til it all goes bad. but shit it's all gud. we threw a party, yeh we threw a party. chicks came over, yeh we threw a party..."
11/4/11 4:30:20: UNkosiyazi: <media omitted>

11/4/11 4:30:26: UNkosiyazi: im still up in the studio editing my Mozambique film. time is 04:30am

11/4/11 5:16:30: Mntwana: "No sleep for the wicked" lol

11/4/11 5:17:31: Mntwana: Can't believe u still up

11/4/11 5:17:52: UNkosiyazi: im up chasing my dreams, they pass me by while im sleeping.

11/4/11 5:43:57: UNkosiyazi: ...jus got home.

11/4/11 5:47:37: Mntwana: Nyt

11/4/11 5:47:52: Mntwana: oh i mean Morning

11/4/11 5:49:41: UNkosiyazi: ps: im a fly-by-night.

11/4/11 5:52:34: Mntwana: Meaning?

11/4/11 5:53:24: UNkosiyazi: night rider.

11/4/11 5:54:42: UNkosiyazi: it must be the coffee i drank midnight but im feelin horny, got a pounding erection.

11/4/11 5:56:05: Mntwana: Cant help u there

11/4/11 6:01:33: UNkosiyazi: it's windy outside too.
11/4/11 7:42:53: Mntwana: "I hear that a first year Wits University
11/4/11 12:12:35: UNkosiyazi: i like that.

11/4/11 12:14:23: Mntwana: The kid is my hero

11/4/11 12:16:50: UNkosiyazi: hahaha...

11/4/11 12:18:15: UNkosiyazi: ...some of these lecturers set exams for students to fail instead of testing if the student(s) understand what was taught in class.

11/4/11 12:19:14: Mntwana: I know all about that..

11/4/11 16:21:42: Mntwana: <media omitted>

11/4/11 16:21:47: Mntwana: Classic lol

11/4/11 19:58:48: UNkosiyazi: every household shuld have one and use it.
11/4/11 20:17:26: UNkosiyazi: how can i want greatness when im afraid of heights?

11/4/11 20:19:11: Mntwana: Who is/was Nkosiyazi?

11/4/11 20:19:43: UNkosiyazi: a Free Thinker

11/5/11 12:53:04: UNkosiyazi: unjani?

11/5/11 13:32:47: UNkosiyazi: Now I Know: Stephen Marley
11/5/11 13:42:50: Mntwana: Im well, a shade lighter, i haven't been outdoors since...dnt recall actually.. if im not studying then im watchng a movie or on my way to the library...i couldn't be better..

11/5/11 13:46:09: UNkosiyazi: <media omitted>

11/5/11 13:46:15: UNkosiyazi: well, alright...

11/5/11 14:00:55: Mntwana: Think i can smell ur food

11/5/11 14:09:24: UNkosiyazi: im so full. uphuthu is the food for man (for me).
11/5/11 18:28:25: UNkosiyazi: craving oven-roasted butternut, chicken, sweetpotato, carrots and potatoes.
11/5/11 18:42:06: Mntwana: Cravings-cravings..

11/5/11 18:43:00: Mntwana: Just decided i wont ask..

11/5/11 18:53:21: UNkosiyazi: hahaha...

11/5/11 20:21:31: UNkosiyazi: Can I go on my way without you
11/5/11 20:26:33: UNkosiyazi: "...ho..." is an exclamation not profanity.

11/5/11 20:28:00: Mntwana: I see...

11/5/11 20:28:33: UNkosiyazi: hahaha...

11/5/11 20:44:05: UNkosiyazi: ps: next time when we get together remember to take full advantage of the opportunity.

11/6/11 2:10:38: Mntwana: *Cough-cough*

11/6/11 8:37:11: UNkosiyazi: excuse the arrogance (confidence).

11/6/11 9:04:32: Mntwana: ...that was the word i was looking for..

11/6/11 10:26:18: UNkosiyazi: uyadelela hhe!

11/6/11 10:41:48: Mntwana: Lol!

11/11/11 11:11:59: UNkosiyazi: 11:11 11.11.11
11/11/11 0:03:58: UNkosiyazi: 11.11.11
11/11/11 0:04:53: Mntwana: Thanx, hope i write well actually..last paper

11/11/11 0:09:33: UNkosiyazi: today?

11/11/11 0:10:11: Mntwana: Yep

11/11/11 0:10:54: UNkosiyazi: write well.

11/11/11 0:11:21: Mntwana: Ng'yabonga

11/11/11 0:19:27: UNkosiyazi: wamukelekile

11/11/11 11:13:02: Mntwana: Ncaaa, thank u, all the same to u..i spent mine writing an exam

11/10/11 23:53:32: Mntwana: 11/11/11

11/14/11 11:50:12: Mntwana: When's yol break starting?

11/14/11 13:24:00: UNkosiyazi: it will start after my 10am exam this cumin Friday.

11/14/11 13:43:24: Mntwana: All the best 4 ur exam(s) then

11/14/11 13:51:51: UNkosiyazi: siyabonga

11/16/11 2:01:31: UNkosiyazi: my upcoming Portuguese film...
11/16/11 2:03:02: Mntwana: Kul, will check it out

11/16/11 12:33:48: Mntwana: Unjani bhuti

11/16/11 12:44:28: UNkosiyazi: hahaha... to answer you, lemme say this:
11/16/11 12:45:56: Mntwana: Lol ok, that says alot *sarcasm*

11/16/11 12:49:05: UNkosiyazi: ...ngingabuye ngithini.

11/16/11 12:51:52: UNkosiyazi: i stay stridin, keep strivin, i seek guidance &like the sun at the dawn i keep risin...

11/16/11 12:52:58: UNkosiyazi: unjani ntomb' enhle?

11/16/11 12:55:42: Mntwana: Thats gud..well im great, as long as i can manage a smile somewhere in the day:)
11/16/11 12:57:53: UNkosiyazi: cute...
11/16/11 12:59:01: Mntwana: No need to explain

11/16/11 12:59:16: UNkosiyazi: okay

11/16/11 13:01:08: Mntwana: And hows yor day

11/16/11 13:21:54: UNkosiyazi: got up about an hour ago, waz up all nyt hustlin like im supposed to.
11/16/11 13:31:35: Mntwana: All rather very interesting..

11/16/11 13:34:23: UNkosiyazi: impilo engayikhetha, angeke ngikhale.

11/16/11 13:35:59: UNkosiyazi: ps: never in my life have i had
females begging me saying they want to have my babies.

11/16/11 13:39:49: Mntwana: U shud b quite pleased about that..

11/16/11 13:42:28: UNkosiyazi: ...just because i sleep with them
doesnt mean i trust them.
11/16/11 13:58:57: Mntwana: U wana have kids wit someone u trust?

11/16/11 14:00:39: UNkosiyazi: someone that the kids will thank me
for choosing her (them) as the mother.

11/16/11 14:01:16: Mntwana: I hear u

11/16/11 14:02:18: UNkosiyazi: it's all for our kids.

11/16/11 14:05:05: Mntwana: At least u got some sense

11/16/11 14:05:51: UNkosiyazi: otherwise, why are we even here?

11/17/11 15:49:59: Mntwana: <media omitted>

11/17/11 15:50:12: Mntwana: A day at wanderes cricket stadium..

11/17/11 15:51:35: Mntwana: <media omitted>

11/17/11 15:52:34: UNkosiyazi: weather looks pretty ¬ depressin...
11/17/11 15:53:33: Mntwana: SA v Australia..twas very hot in fact..

11/17/11 16:00:18: UNkosiyazi: thanks for sharing.

11/17/11 16:00:55: Mntwana: Sure

11/17/11 16:12:14: UNkosiyazi: im thinkin bout SA.

11/17/11 16:13:47: Mntwana: Oh really now..anything specific bwt it?

11/17/11 16:15:53: UNkosiyazi: vibe, weather and its stress.

11/17/11 16:16:38: Mntwana: Haha, it's "stress"

11/17/11 16:17:23: UNkosiyazi: yeah, its stress.

11/17/11 16:18:11: Mntwana: You must "come back home..."
11/17/11 16:19:20: UNkosiyazi: hahaha...
11/17/11 16:20:55: Mntwana: Lol, i hear u..
11/17/11 16:22:19: UNkosiyazi: peace peace be still...

11/17/11 17:46:13: UNkosiyazi: <media omitted>

11/18/11 8:22:33: Mntwana: Thought something was different about your
picture, until it came to me...
11/18/11 8:39:01: UNkosiyazi: so observant...

11/18/11 8:40:14: Mntwana: Lol, analysis is a skill..

11/18/11 8:40:40: UNkosiyazi: cute

11/18/11 8:46:02: Mntwana: A good morning to u.

11/18/11 9:10:59: Mntwana: Ubhale kahle

11/18/11 11:50:13: UNkosiyazi: ngibhale kahle impela, ngiyabonga.

11/18/11 15:03:07: Mntwana: Kul:)

11/18/11 21:15:30: UNkosiyazi: <media omitted>

11/18/11 21:15:37: UNkosiyazi: missing amawings...

11/18/11 21:56:14: UNkosiyazi: <media omitted>

11/18/11 21:56:19: UNkosiyazi: my food (rooibos tea, wings, rice, potatoes w/Mayo) is ready.

11/20/11 3:28:39: UNkosiyazi: "Girls, I ask em do they smoke?
11/20/11 18:07:24: Mntwana: Tried checking owt ur video using the link u sent an it gave me some msg bwt waiting coz the video is nt available

11/20/11 18:10:20: UNkosiyazi: http://t.co/THhsqV49

11/20/11 18:17:25: Mntwana: Totaly attracted to subtitles all of a sudden..
11/20/11 18:18:31: UNkosiyazi: what do you mean?
11/20/11 18:25:31: Mntwana: Yea i mean the fact that the language is foreign to me..
11/20/11 18:27:12: UNkosiyazi: hahaha...
11/20/11 18:31:01: Mntwana: Lol, oh really now...mncm..

11/20/11 18:31:57: UNkosiyazi: angiqambi amanga.

11/20/11 18:53:07: Mntwana: Wateva u say

11/20/11 18:54:19: UNkosiyazi: hah!

11/20/11 18:56:19: UNkosiyazi: by the way, that film is going to be ground breaking in all sense.
11/20/11 18:56:39: UNkosiyazi: what are you up so late doing?

11/20/11 18:56:54: Mntwana: Hahaha testimony!

11/20/11 18:58:05: Mntwana: I was doing some packing, ryt nw im just surfing the net. Nthng serious

11/20/11 18:58:22: UNkosiyazi: tryna lighten up the situation, cant be ever militant or "serious".

11/20/11 18:58:57: Mntwana: Im glad thats coming from u

11/20/11 18:59:05: UNkosiyazi: enjoy the packing, if there is anything to be enjoyed.

11/20/11 18:59:42: Mntwana: Not at all, i need 5 gentleman to help me out really

11/20/11 19:01:07: UNkosiyazi: gentle is gay / soft, dont u need real man / strong?

11/20/11 19:01:48: Mntwana: Oh well, that then! Lol

11/20/11 19:01:49: UNkosiyazi: one will do more than what these five "soft" ones would.

11/20/11 19:02:15: UNkosiyazi: im so full of it- hahaha...

11/20/11 19:02:18: Mntwana: Haha, u over analysing now

11/20/11 19:03:08: UNkosiyazi: maybe...
11/20/11 20:15:33: UNkosiyazi: <media omitted>

11/21/11 1:18:15: UNkosiyazi: Same Ole Love: Anita Baker
11/22/11 2:36:41: Mntwana: Goodness gracious...that pic

11/22/11 2:37:13: UNkosiyazi: what pic?

11/22/11 2:37:53: Mntwana: The last one u sent

11/22/11 2:38:32: UNkosiyazi: oh, that one! what about it?

11/22/11 2:40:33: Mntwana: Lol, it's kul

11/22/11 2:49:01: UNkosiyazi: u mean da pic or u mean u dont wanna talkabout it?

11/22/11 3:35:49: Mntwana: The pic. u rather a lil' slow today hmm..

11/22/11 9:47:23: UNkosiyazi: guess so.

11/22/11 9:49:30: Mntwana: And i thought u wud argue otherwise

11/22/11 10:01:18: UNkosiyazi: hahaha...
11/22/11 10:34:11: Mntwana: I guess so

11/22/11 11:05:46: UNkosiyazi: anyway, im glad u r infactuated with my poster picture.

11/22/11 14:24:18: Mntwana: Hahaha, na, im nt infatuated at all!

11/22/11 15:30:43: UNkosiyazi: oh well, cant blame a brother for trying.

11/22/11 15:48:09: Mntwana: Lol, u sure were trying...

11/22/11 16:11:30: UNkosiyazi: hah!

11/23/11 6:53:04: UNkosiyazi: Girls, I ask em do they smoke?
11/23/11 7:49:19: UNkosiyazi: is there a way you can get me the track titled JIKWA IMALI by Magesh (Tokollo)?

11/23/11 11:07:00: Mntwana: Uhr....ay, i dnt think so coz the people i cud ask have went home already

11/23/11 11:35:20: Mntwana: U didn't by any chance dial my number today?

11/23/11 11:43:34: UNkosiyazi: hahaha...

11/23/11 11:44:26: Mntwana: Wats so funny, im just asking

11/23/11 11:45:26: Mntwana: i got a voice msg 4rm a pvt no. and i dnt recognize the voice

11/23/11 11:45:55: UNkosiyazi: ...out of the people, why me?

11/23/11 11:46:51: Mntwana: U matched sum clues

11/23/11 11:47:14: Mntwana: I neva recognize ur voice on the fone

11/23/11 11:47:20: Mntwana: U zulu

11/23/11 11:47:39: Mntwana: And u call wit a pvt no.

11/23/11 12:00:37: UNkosiyazi: funny...
11/23/11 12:02:45: Mntwana: Why aren't u certain that it wasn't u

11/23/11 12:11:33: UNkosiyazi: coz in life there are no certainties.

11/23/11 12:14:44: Mntwana: U really just being smart with me nw

11/23/11 12:28:00: UNkosiyazi: am i?

11/23/11 12:31:25: Mntwana: Yep

11/23/11 12:43:33: UNkosiyazi: how so Mntwana?

11/23/11 14:08:31: Mntwana: Noma ungasa phendulanga akusenani, im quite sure i figured owt who my mystery caller is

11/23/11 15:31:53: UNkosiyazi: hahaha...

11/23/11 23:20:08: UNkosiyazi: <media omitted>

11/23/11 23:20:18: UNkosiyazi: Thanksgiving

11/24/11 13:53:48: Mntwana: Lol, thats quite a thanksgiving!

11/24/11 16:00:08: UNkosiyazi: ...indeed.

11/24/11 21:19:15: UNkosiyazi: bottle after bottle till i get messed up.

11/24/11 21:58:01: UNkosiyazi: tell me, what's that song about Tkzee "ela ngwana wa ka..."?

11/25/11 4:32:36: Mntwana: Cnt think of the melody of the song so i can try remember the lyrics

11/26/11 1:24:13: UNkosiyazi: good morning!

11/26/11 1:38:38: Mntwana: Dankie:) morning to u too

11/26/11 1:39:57: UNkosiyazi: ngiyazibongela.

11/27/11 1:39:58: UNkosiyazi: how did you sleep?

11/27/11 2:56:46: Mntwana: im visiting emakhaya @Mangweni, MP..doing community outreach projects..

11/27/11 2:57:22: Mntwana: i dnt sleep so well on the floor

11/27/11 7:50:57: UNkosiyazi: give it time, you'll get used to it.

11/28/11 0:23:16: UNkosiyazi: goodmorning!
11/28/11 2:22:56: Mntwana: Aren't u sweet...thanx

11/28/11 6:58:25: UNkosiyazi: you're welcome.
11/28/11 7:02:21: Mntwana: Its great. Makes me so happy to be with the people and they're so welcoming:D
11/28/11 7:10:10: UNkosiyazi: im glad you're contributing to social programs. what do you have to do there?

11/28/11 8:27:34: Mntwana: Clothes distribution, academic excellence workshops, we visit primary/hyskuls an interact with the kids and provide information on studying further, volunteering at the orphanages n hospitals..etc

11/28/11 8:31:38: Mntwana: I do a bit in terms of social programs, it's fulfilling. Teaches u to have a compassionate heart. And the joy that the people express 4rm wat we do is just classic:)

11/28/11 8:38:28: Mntwana: We visited this other house today and there was a very old granny who cnt walk, she
11/28/11 8:51:22: Mntwana: <media omitted>

11/28/11 11:20:04: UNkosiyazi: interestin...

11/29/11 1:04:34: UNkosiyazi: "i just cant believe that you've been sent to me from above. you're my angel of love. i cant wait to feel your sunshine..."
11/29/11 1:19:37: UNkosiyazi: im listenin to it while sippin Southern Comfort...

11/29/11 1:19:50: UNkosiyazi: <media omitted>

11/29/11 3:28:48: Mntwana: Tried googling the lyrics?

11/29/11 14:43:58: UNkosiyazi:
http://www.realtor.com/blogs/2011/11/23/bruce-willis-lists-idaho-home-photos/

11/29/11 16:32:37: Mntwana: Great stuff:)

11/29/11 16:37:19: UNkosiyazi: hah!

11/29/11 16:39:48: UNkosiyazi: <media omitted>

11/29/11 16:39:53: UNkosiyazi: detoxing...

11/29/11 16:41:21: Mntwana: Kahle bo! Detox nge-Heineken?

11/29/11 16:42:37: UNkosiyazi: gotta tone down Southern Comfort.

11/30/11 16:05:52: UNkosiyazi: Classic material indeed...
http://yourblackwoman.blogspot.com/2011/12/meet-sara-bartman-
original-video-vixen.html#more

12/1/11 15:15:15: UNkosiyazi: A spiritually evolved woman understands
the difference between chasing men and choosing a husband. The
difference has a profound effect on the quality of life for her, her
offspring and her community. Strong married couples build wealthy
families which, in turn, build affluent communities. When the
majority of babies are born to single individuals, or into marriages
that don‚Äôt last, you can‚Äôt sustain an economically sound
community. There is a lack of physical comfort because we are not
pooling resources. People are fighting over child support and
stretching one income among several households.

12/2/11 1:26:32: UNkosiyazi: how did you sleep?

12/2/11 1:35:50: Mntwana: Mosquitos are just having a ball on my
skin..
12/2/11 1:36:29: Mntwana: ie. I didnt sleep so great

12/2/11 1:37:56: UNkosiyazi: you should just let the mosquitos numb
your skin by eating you too much, that's what i do when im in
Mozambique.

12/2/11 2:03:13: Mntwana: Dont sound like gud advice

12/2/11 2:07:49: UNkosiyazi: hah!

12/2/11 2:28:03: Mntwana: Ja, u just want me to die 4rm malaria

12/2/11 2:29:10: UNkosiyazi: hhawu Nkosi yami, ngingayifisa kanjani-nje into embi kanje?

12/2/11 2:31:19: Mntwana: Ur implying it, akudingeki ukuthi ukufise

12/2/11 2:32:13: UNkosiyazi: hhawu, ayidle izibekele bo.

12/2/11 15:09:06: UNkosiyazi: <media omitted>

12/2/11 15:26:39: Mntwana: Where u off to

12/2/11 15:27:55: UNkosiyazi: what do u mean?

12/2/11 15:28:43: Mntwana: U walking in ur video..

12/2/11 15:29:07: UNkosiyazi: ...to the studio.

12/2/11 15:46:00: UNkosiyazi: <media omitted>

12/2/11 15:48:17: Mntwana: With the way u dressed, seems pretty cold

12/2/11 15:49:39: UNkosiyazi: minus two

12/2/11 15:58:11: Mntwana: Cud be worse..

12/2/11 15:58:51: UNkosiyazi: yeah, change of season

12/3/11 0:03:41: UNkosiyazi: mornin! is it a gud one or what?
12/3/11 3:42:35: Mntwana: Late night movies at the cinema in nelspruit, otherwise was traveling throughout the night..

12/3/11 3:43:56: Mntwana: An yea it's a gud morning sure..
12/3/11 9:58:20: UNkosiyazi: it's a good one for me indeed, just barely got up.

12/3/11 9:58:47: UNkosiyazi: what about the word "mango"?

12/3/11 12:08:06: Mntwana: Im missing a mango in my life!

12/3/11 12:09:34: UNkosiyazi: hahaha...
12/3/11 15:34:41: UNkosiyazi: Lay down here beside me and we‚Äôll
cruise the caravan
12/3/11 15:55:15: Mntwana: It sure is..

12/4/11 12:54:52: UNkosiyazi: <media omitted>

12/4/11 12:54:58: UNkosiyazi: howaz yo day?
12/4/11 13:08:37: UNkosiyazi: <media omitted>

12/4/11 14:52:27: Mntwana: I just over-slept..slept thru half the
afternoon an just woke up. Guess i wont b sleeping tonyt

12/4/11 14:54:19: Mntwana: Thats a cute pic...
12/4/11 15:02:09: UNkosiyazi: gud2kno...
12/4/11 15:07:01: Mntwana: Ya. Wasn't getn much sleep while doing
it..
12/4/11 15:08:03: Mntwana: How r are u?
12/4/11 15:12:57: UNkosiyazi: still on vacation, skul starts first
week of January, im just kickin it, doin this and that...
12/4/11 15:32:26: Mntwana: 8Days..
12/4/11 15:43:55: UNkosiyazi: cool

12/4/11 18:19:33: UNkosiyazi: my snuff supply is getting depleted,
can you mail me some more?

12/5/11 12:13:58: UNkosiyazi: my snuff supply is getting depleted,
can you mail me some more?

12/5/11 12:18:49: UNkosiyazi: As in the stuff in the blue and yellow
container?

12/5/11 12:20:21: Mntwana: I know wat snuff is..

12/5/11 12:35:31: UNkosiyazi: i use it to talk to my grandmothers
when i leave the house or wherever i am. it's like a rosary or thusby
that reminds me to pray (talk) to my caregivers (ancestors).
12/5/11 12:37:32: UNkosiyazi: remember, even when you drink your fav
beverages to spill some for them too.
12/5/11 12:49:10: UNkosiyazi: listen and learn, you gonna be a mother
and a wife someday, hopefully. you gonna be a granny, God willing.
you definately gonna be an ancestor, you dont have a choice.

12/5/11 13:08:48: Mntwana: Sermon..

12/5/11 13:18:44: UNkosiyazi: free church service

12/6/11 23:23:42: UNkosiyazi: i like this Luther song:
Wednesday, December 7, 2011
12/7/11 0:23:57: Mntwana: BComm,Wits--->checküëç

12/7/11 0:24:48: Mntwana: Gosh im so happy and yet relieved:D

12/7/11 0:29:54: UNkosiyazi: you should Give Thanks however you /
your family does it.
12/7/11 0:31:28: Mntwana: Sure-sure..thank you:)

12/7/11 0:38:59: UNkosiyazi: where are you studying next year?

12/7/11 0:57:29: Mntwana: Just need confirmation ryt now, otherwise
im moving up to dbn..

12/7/11 9:03:27: Mntwana: I wouldn't buy anyone tobacco or alcohol
and i wouldn't feel comfortable doing it for u either..
12/7/11 10:58:53: UNkosiyazi: okay

12/7/11 11:18:05: UNkosiyazi: seems like it is going to be a good
show for the Emerging Black Middle Class on SABC1:
12/7/11 11:32:02: Mntwana: What's your source?

12/7/11 11:45:07: UNkosiyazi: bunch of sources: UCT Uniliver
Institute of Marketing is one of them.

12/7/11 11:54:40: Mntwana: Kul, shocking numbers..but makes sense,
people spend what they dont have and it wud take alot 4 that to
change

12/7/11 11:58:03: Mntwana: I wud have thought though that the rate of
vehicle repossession wud have declined by now coz our economy is in a
state of recovery..

12/7/11 11:58:26: Mntwana: Hence i was asking bwt ur source

12/7/11 12:18:40: UNkosiyazi: cool

12/7/11 12:19:03: UNkosiyazi: Philadelphia D.A. Drops Death Penalty
Against Mumia Abu-Jamal
12/7/11 12:31:21: UNkosiyazi: FREE MUMIA!
12/7/11 15:44:09: Mntwana: Ay, ya ne..

12/7/11 20:19:45: UNkosiyazi: yeah, we must fight for our freedom
fighters!

12/7/11 20:20:01: UNkosiyazi: <media omitted>

12/7/11 20:31:44: UNkosiyazi: i did a film about President Zuma
before he came into power, and i have never showed it to anyone. im
wondering if time is right for me to release it now or should i wait
until end of next year?
12/7/11 23:39:07: Mntwana: Why end of next year?

12/7/11 23:39:25: Mntwana: Stunning foto

12/7/11 23:44:55: UNkosiyazi: ngiyazibongela ngesithombe.

12/7/11 23:45:45: UNkosiyazi: im thinkin by then the time will be right since i've been wanting to show the public since 2008.

12/7/11 23:47:34: Mntwana: I hear u...quite interesting

12/7/11 23:55:54: UNkosiyazi: <media omitted>

12/7/11 23:57:12: UNkosiyazi: a teaser... hah!

12/8/11 0:05:11: Mntwana: Definitely a teaser. I like.

12/8/11 0:09:03: UNkosiyazi: <media omitted>

12/8/11 0:09:42: UNkosiyazi: hahaha...

12/8/11 0:11:32: UNkosiyazi: <media omitted>

12/8/11 0:18:02: Mntwana: Thanx 4 those

12/8/11 0:22:49: UNkosiyazi: <media omitted>

12/8/11 0:24:30: UNkosiyazi: hah!

12/8/11 2:26:26: UNkosiyazi: some dreams stay dreams and others dreams come true.

12/8/11 2:27:42: UNkosiyazi: Liquid Deep says: "...never let go of your dreams. no matter how hard it may seem."
12/8/11 6:12:01: Mntwana: I love liquiDeep, gud house ryt there

12/8/11 10:54:58: UNkosiyazi: yep!

12/8/11 15:40:26: Mntwana: <media omitted>

12/8/11 15:40:36: Mntwana: An amateur rehearsal wit fwens

12/8/11 18:44:21: UNkosiyazi: ya'll are / were having a great time!

12/9/11 0:38:58: Mntwana: Yep:)

12/10/11 0:45:34: UNkosiyazi: <media omitted>

12/10/11 0:45:36: UNkosiyazi: gudmornin!

12/10/11 0:49:47: Mntwana: Morning UNkosiyazi:)

12/10/11 0:50:40: Mntwana: Lol, wats up wit em' oreos

12/10/11 2:34:05: UNkosiyazi: im enjoyin the Obamas...

12/10/11 3:06:40: Mntwana: Obama's?

12/10/11 3:59:14: UNkosiyazi: yep, Oreo = Coconut

12/10/11 12:51:47: UNkosiyazi: AmaPantsula Ajabulile = Professor ft
Kabelo
12/10/11 12:59:38: UNkosiyazi: you like Ungazoba Serious = Big NUZ?

12/10/11 13:03:55: Mntwana: Im into durban kwaito by all means, bt im
not up to date ryt nw

12/10/11 13:04:32: UNkosiyazi: hahaha...

12/11/11 13:18:50: UNkosiyazi: <media omitted>

12/11/11 14:58:55: UNkosiyazi: ulale kahle

12/11/11 17:15:01: UNkosiyazi: <media omitted>

12/12/11 1:09:36: UNkosiyazi: how did you sleep?
12/12/11 2:01:02: Mntwana: Lol, ur videos are amusing

12/12/11 2:01:28: Mntwana: i slept well thanx..slept alot in fact

12/12/11 2:03:44: Mntwana: Like the song playing in the background

12/12/11 9:23:29: UNkosiyazi: Lady Gaga.
12/12/11 9:31:01: UNkosiyazi: it's minus six degrees outside.

12/12/11 9:41:20: Mntwana: Twas just last nyt, i cudnt get myself to wake up

12/12/11 9:41:39: Mntwana: Thats just very cold!

12/12/11 9:43:30: UNkosiyazi: hahaha... maybe you needed to learn something from your dreams.
12/12/11 9:44:22: UNkosiyazi: ...what's funny is that it is sunny and all but extremely cold.

12/12/11 9:44:23: Mntwana: Well, i had a sweet dream, so maybe..

12/12/11 9:45:03: UNkosiyazi: you learn anything from your amathongo?

12/12/11 9:46:19: Mntwana: U mean generally, or specifically on the most recent one?

12/12/11 9:46:38: UNkosiyazi: most recent one!

12/12/11 9:48:07: Mntwana: Well...4rm the little that i remember, it was more about me imparting knowledge to young kids.

12/12/11 9:49:09: Mntwana: So i wudnt quite say i learnt something, i woke up a lil surprised

12/12/11 9:50:25: UNkosiyazi: great stuff, she is a teacher.
12/12/11 9:53:37: Mntwana: Who is "she"?
12/12/11 9:58:22: UNkosiyazi: you is "she"!
12/12/11 9:58:55: UNkosiyazi: writings are on the wall!

12/12/11 10:01:56: Mntwana: Lol..blonde in disguise..

12/12/11 10:05:25: UNkosiyazi: hah!
12/12/11 10:06:26: Mntwana: Who u quoting?

12/12/11 10:06:54: UNkosiyazi: Erykah Badu

12/12/11 10:12:05: UNkosiyazi: it inspires me this Erykah Badu song:
12/12/11 10:17:25: Mntwana: Like the lyrics

12/12/11 10:20:37: UNkosiyazi: i love them...
12/12/11 10:51:39: UNkosiyazi: in my dream last night, a woman was teaching me some deep doctrine and showing me some signs: i dont really recollect it all but i believe it was a sign of things to come that i will learn.
12/12/11 13:38:16: Mntwana: Interesting one

12/12/11 13:53:49: UNkosiyazi: Meet Sara Bartman: The Original Video Vixen
12/13/11 15:11:49: UNkosiyazi: before you lay yourself down to sleep tonight, know that im glad i know you and wish you well in all your dreams.

12/13/11 22:53:15: UNkosiyazi: "To just spend all my time
12/14/11 0:07:57: Mntwana: Oh wow, thats nice to know

12/14/11 0:15:40: UNkosiyazi: anytime...
12/14/11 3:27:20: UNkosiyazi: <media omitted>

12/14/11 3:27:26: UNkosiyazi: five Corona's, im feeling nice.

12/14/11 3:29:54: Mntwana: Angeke uhlale ungabi "mnandi"

12/14/11 3:31:00: UNkosiyazi: hahaha... what can i do baby, it's festive.

12/14/11 3:32:38: Mntwana: I dont see the difrence really, noma ngabe ifestive, noma kungeyona ibhodlela lona liminjalo

12/14/11 3:37:12: UNkosiyazi: okay, lemme rephrase: i work hard and play hard. hhawu, haven't you seen the Stout or Black Label or Ijuba adverts? they show men working hard and playing hard. hahaha...
12/14/11 3:37:38: UNkosiyazi: just blow me a kiss Mntwana.

12/14/11 3:38:04: Mntwana: Hahahahaha, cha uphuze ngempela

12/14/11 3:38:55: Mntwana: Yikho nje usungikhumbhula

12/14/11 3:39:21: UNkosiyazi: hhayi wena, akushiwo ukuthi ubaba uphuzile noma udakiwe, kuthiwa ubaba ujabulile.

12/14/11 3:40:31: UNkosiyazi: ...ngikukhumbula mihla namalanga wena Mntwana. phela uyintombi yami, ungangenzeli amaflop lapho, uyangizwa?

12/14/11 3:43:21: Mntwana: Hhehe..uyangiqeda

12/14/11 3:44:41: UNkosiyazi: kanjani nje kodwa?

12/14/11 3:47:18: UNkosiyazi: okay, uyangiziba? kulungile, love dont live here anymore.

12/14/11 3:48:21: UNkosiyazi: anyway, im excited coz i re-started (resumed) my Zulu novel today.

12/14/11 3:50:47: Mntwana: Ngisematasa ngomsebenzi wasendlini, ngizok'naka kungek'dala

12/14/11 3:55:53: UNkosiyazi: hahaha...
12/14/11 3:56:02: UNkosiyazi: <media omitted>

12/14/11 3:59:36: Mntwana: I gues by the time im done, ul be down and out

12/14/11 4:01:16: UNkosiyazi: ...never!

12/14/11 4:01:49: UNkosiyazi: i'll probably go take a shower and start writing.

12/14/11 4:02:24: Mntwana: Im done anyway

12/14/11 4:02:34: UNkosiyazi: ...should have about 150 pages by the end of this year. im a workaholic.

12/14/11 4:02:57: UNkosiyazi: im doing seven pages per day. i will leave a mark on this planet earth.

12/14/11 4:03:11: Mntwana: 150pages of what?

12/14/11 4:03:29: UNkosiyazi: Zulu novel

12/14/11 4:05:31: Mntwana: Oh u writing one?

12/14/11 4:07:35: UNkosiyazi: im always writing: creative, academic and otherwise.

12/14/11 4:11:24: Mntwana: "AmaFlop" lol..

12/14/11 4:14:31: UNkosiyazi: exactly, ungazongibhanqa nezimpuphu zangakini.

12/14/11 4:14:41: UNkosiyazi: <media omitted>

12/14/11 4:18:10: Mntwana: Haha, buka nje ukuthi "ujabule" kanjani

12/14/11 4:18:45: Mntwana: Hahahahahaha

12/14/11 4:19:20: UNkosiyazi: ngiqinisile, uhlekani?

12/14/11 4:19:47: Mntwana: ur us

12/14/11 4:20:11: Mntwana: ur use of words..

12/14/11 4:21:12: UNkosiyazi: what about my use of words?

12/14/11 4:24:55: Mntwana: correct me if im wrong, but I dont
remember any explicit agreement between u and I..

12/14/11 4:29:02: UNkosiyazi: it doesn't matter if it was pronounced
or not, what matters is that it was assumed.

12/14/11 4:32:49: Mntwana: I dont do assumptions

12/14/11 4:47:05: UNkosiyazi: kanti what is me and you doing? ours
was "concluded".

12/14/11 5:03:48: UNkosiyazi: what am i trying to prove? it's five in
the morning, im off to sleep.

12/14/11 5:08:50: Mntwana: Sleep well

12/14/11 5:09:55: UNkosiyazi: will do. thank you very much. got lot
of work to do today.

12/14/11 5:10:42: UNkosiyazi: ps: me and you are murderers, we kill
time. are we friends or an item?

12/14/11 5:11:34: Mntwana: How about u go to sleep, il answer that
question later

12/14/11 10:14:49: Mntwana: We friends

12/14/11 11:16:55: UNkosiyazi: hahahaha....

12/14/11 12:36:43: Mntwana: Wats so funny?

12/14/11 14:12:53: UNkosiyazi: "we friends" thing.

12/14/11 14:24:46: Mntwana: Well i aint doing any business with you, neither am i a relative of urs and let me make this clear, i will have no man thinking that he can "screw me" and fulfill his sexual fantasies about me, just 4 the heck of it..an i take offence in you using the word "screw". I have values that i uphold and im a lady with self-respect...

12/14/11 14:25:22: UNkosiyazi: point taken.

12/14/11 14:47:48: UNkosiyazi: <media omitted>

12/14/11 15:06:54: Mntwana: I dont follow wat the article is about

12/14/11 15:53:22: UNkosiyazi: it's a Bob Marley beverage owned by his family that calms you down.

12/15/11 0:34:39: Mntwana: I wonder if weed isn't one of the main ingredients...weed calms u down, doesn't it?

12/15/11 5:39:50: UNkosiyazi: yeah, weed is good but this drink doesnt have it, it only has the ingredients highlighted on the right.

12/17/11 22:04:00: UNkosiyazi: <media omitted>

12/18/11 1:27:51: Mntwana: Thats a smoky hi....

12/18/11 2:02:30: UNkosiyazi: hey...

12/18/11 6:18:57: Mntwana: Hi UNkosiyazi

12/18/11 12:19:42: UNkosiyazi: Hi Mntwanasenkosi!

12/18/11 12:20:26: Mntwana: Unjani bhuti:)

12/18/11 12:21:51: UNkosiyazi: besides work, im gud. unjani wena?

12/18/11 12:24:14: Mntwana: Oh im great, just tryna win a game of ten-pin bowling

12/18/11 12:27:21: UNkosiyazi: good luck or rather, enjoy it.

12/18/11 12:27:30: UNkosiyazi: pics?

12/18/11 12:29:10: Mntwana: <media omitted>

12/18/11 12:29:15: Mntwana: Im bloody 2nd

12/18/11 12:29:58: Mntwana: Nt bad 4 someone who was on nil for 3 rounds..

12/18/11 12:31:11: Mntwana: bt i just decided to put matters into my own hands and walk up to those pins and bamn, i had a strike:D

12/18/11 12:33:28: Mntwana: Im avoiding taking fotos with me in them, got a "lil" sunburnt..

12/18/11 12:38:07: UNkosiyazi: hah!

12/18/11 12:40:37: Mntwana: Lol..

12/18/11 15:10:57: Mntwana: <media omitted>

12/18/11 15:19:00: UNkosiyazi: sounds like ya'll are having fun.

12/18/11 15:49:11: Mntwana: Yea, 16 different minds are quite something..fun is inevitable in this case

12/18/11 16:09:36: UNkosiyazi: nice one

12/19/11 1:20:25: UNkosiyazi: ...dont tell me you are still sleepin! rise and shine, it's a new day. enjoy it.

12/19/11 1:24:09: Mntwana: lol, Just came out of the bath tub..im up, thanx

12/19/11 1:24:51: UNkosiyazi: did u hav to paint such a picture?

12/19/11 1:26:14: Mntwana: R u kidding me, lol, ay bengingazi

12/19/11 1:31:25: UNkosiyazi: oh really, ubungazi? that is funny.

12/19/11 1:32:11: UNkosiyazi: im kiddin...
12/19/11 1:33:59: Mntwana: Angithi yols minds work overtime..
12/19/11 1:36:06: UNkosiyazi: hahaha...
12/19/11 1:38:36: Mntwana: It's definitely sad, especially 4 us who believe in the institution of marriage

12/19/11 1:41:44: UNkosiyazi: ive concluded that for me, im just gonna find someone who just wanna put family before career. there turn to be unnecessary competition when both r pushing career coz family (children) get compromised under the guise of "children are expensive".

12/19/11 1:42:56: UNkosiyazi: the problem is bigger than this. there is more to it.

12/19/11 1:51:30: Mntwana: It doesnt seem like an issue 4 me for people to seek a career b4 family

12/19/11 1:52:34: Mntwana: Once u got a career established, then kul, priorities can change again to family first

12/19/11 1:53:21: UNkosiyazi: in average, how long does it take to establish career?

12/19/11 1:54:36: Mntwana: Depends..il think of mine, a gud 5yrs afta honours

12/19/11 1:59:15: UNkosiyazi: which means if all goes accordingly, 28 years you are starting to have kids?

12/19/11 2:04:17: Mntwana: Preferrably b4 then, bt im in no hurry to have kids, so even 28 wudnt b a train smash. As long as im nt single at that age

12/19/11 2:06:01: UNkosiyazi: hahaha...

12/19/11 2:06:08: UNkosiyazi: it is silly, a man wants a lot of children and wants their mother to be there for them (housewife).
12/19/11 2:07:14: Mntwana: Not house wife forever darling

12/19/11 2:10:51: Mntwana: I also believe in being there for my kids and raising them myself..

12/19/11 2:11:29: UNkosiyazi: im a hard man, traditional and cultured. no way im going to do western marriage. im going traditional. she will not only marry me but my family also. if she cant get along with them, she'll have to ship out. leave my grannies children behind.
12/19/11 2:13:38: Mntwana: Will respond to this later, getting a hairwash at the salon..

12/19/11 2:15:04: UNkosiyazi: peace!

12/19/11 2:25:59: UNkosiyazi: ps: the CNN guy is crying over the fact that Kobe Bryant's wife is gonna part with half of Kobe's millions, joint custody of the children and alimony.
12/19/11 2:32:09: UNkosiyazi: traditional marriage is the way to protect the interests of the children.

12/19/11 2:47:00: UNkosiyazi: what does she want to do with my property? my brothers are the ones to look after my property when im gone, not umfazi. they look after my property and children until my male children are grown ukuvusa umuzi wami (uyise wabo).

12/19/11 6:06:54: Mntwana: I think the issue there on cnn is really a legal issue that could have been avoided from the beginning of the marriage..

12/19/11 6:12:36: Mntwana: And what u saying whether it's traditional or not, appears to undermine the fact that we women also want to protect the children and their interests. Why shud ur brothers take care of the children?
12/19/11 6:14:03: Mntwana: It's either i dont undastand or im a lil' hard-headed, eitherway, this doesn't make sense to me

12/19/11 10:21:46: UNkosiyazi: ...because the children doesn't belong to the woman nor to a man but to the man's ancestors.

12/19/11 22:37:07: UNkosiyazi: im still feelin this Drake track:
12/19/11 22:37:52: UNkosiyazi: Patience is a Virtue that is only possessed by a few.

12/19/11 23:11:38: UNkosiyazi: i feel creative juices tonight so lemme share a piece i've just thought about:
12/20/11 0:39:19: Mntwana: Great piece, totaly adore it

12/20/11 0:46:21: UNkosiyazi: thank you

12/20/11 13:21:47: UNkosiyazi: <media omitted>

12/20/11 13:25:53: Mntwana: For a second there, it did not look like u in the picture

12/20/11 14:00:12: UNkosiyazi: hah! it looked like who?

12/20/11 14:01:03: Mntwana: A look-alike of yourself

12/20/11 14:01:34: Mntwana: Perhaps a sibling

12/20/11 14:01:40: UNkosiyazi: hahaha...

12/20/11 14:42:29: UNkosiyazi: before i forget and get caught up, lemme say: enjoy your festive season (in Zulu it's called Ishwama / feast of the first fruits or harvest)!

12/20/11 14:47:13: Mntwana: Oh why thank you
12/20/11 14:53:35: UNkosiyazi: love the green heart, just finished eating a bloody liver w/carrots and milk.

12/20/11 14:54:18: Mntwana: Bloody liver?

12/20/11 14:57:30: UNkosiyazi: i can only eat it while it's still bloody so i can get the iron. can't eat it when it is "rubbery."

12/20/11 15:03:11: Mntwana: Did it ever go through the fire?

12/20/11 15:04:36: UNkosiyazi: it does but barely. i dip it in and out on oil under high heat.

12/20/11 15:05:34: Mntwana: Mhm..ay cha..

12/20/11 15:08:44: UNkosiyazi: what is the point of eating good / healthy food when we kill its nutrients by the way we prepare it?
12/20/11 15:10:33: UNkosiyazi: when i grew up there was a food chart in the house mounted on the fridge and you had to make sure in a day you took your daily servings in all ranges of food.

12/20/11 15:11:14: UNkosiyazi: males i kno think it is crazy to eat any meal without meat.

12/20/11 15:11:57: UNkosiyazi: i often judge them by saying: bakhula belamba that's why.

12/20/11 15:25:03: Mntwana: Lol thats funny. I hear u though, im not a fan of veggies so i "disguise" them..
12/20/11 15:27:36: UNkosiyazi: disguise them or kill them? hahaha...
12/20/11 15:33:24: Mntwana: Lol, both..
12/20/11 16:06:55: Mntwana: Uma umuntu ethi:"Uqhuba intwala ngewisa"

12/20/11 18:14:46: UNkosiyazi: uyachwensa / uyadelela.

12/21/11 3:15:27: Mntwana: Thanks lol..

12/21/11 3:59:54: UNkosiyazi: <media omitted>

12/21/11 4:12:40: Mntwana: U not bored maybe?

12/21/11 5:37:40: UNkosiyazi: honestly, im never bored.

12/21/11 5:54:01: Mntwana: I've heard/read that lecture before. So ja, i know

12/21/11 6:07:59: UNkosiyazi: hahaha...

12/21/11 20:08:27: UNkosiyazi: <media omitted>

12/21/11 23:42:31: UNkosiyazi: <media omitted>

12/22/11 0:10:03: UNkosiyazi: i love sleeping on the floor...

12/22/11 9:05:09: Mntwana: So u always say..

12/22/11 9:06:24: Mntwana: Got my guy friends cooking us supper today

12/22/11 9:14:35: UNkosiyazi: interesting...

12/22/11 9:18:28: Mntwana: Angithi bayavilapha, so if they want food from us, they'll help us make that food

12/22/11 9:21:15: UNkosiyazi: angithule.

12/22/11 9:23:13: Mntwana: Lol

12/22/11 9:23:23: Mntwana: thula bhuti

12/22/11 9:34:40: UNkosiyazi: im just too picky on which battles i fight.

12/22/11 9:35:28: Mntwana: An thats a gud thing

12/22/11 9:42:51: UNkosiyazi: funny...

12/23/11 2:17:43: Mntwana: Heard em' tracks: ungazoba serious & amapantsula ajabulile

12/23/11 2:19:41: UNkosiyazi: nice ones hey?

12/23/11 2:21:50: Mntwana: I've never been disappointed by Professor & Big Nuz

12/23/11 2:24:17: UNkosiyazi: good

12/23/11 2:25:55: Mntwana: I had a driving lesson with my dad...ngifile ukuthethiswa

12/23/11 2:27:05: UNkosiyazi: u just had it this morning?

12/23/11 2:27:36: Mntwana: Na, this week

12/23/11 2:28:23: UNkosiyazi: howiz da progress?

12/23/11 2:29:14: Mntwana: Im a fast learner..lol, an hour was long

12/23/11 2:32:47: UNkosiyazi: great... better your father is teaching you. im all for fatherhood and support.

12/23/11 2:33:47: Mntwana: But someone once said to me, that i shudnt get either a boyfriend or dad to teach me how to
12/23/11 2:34:18: Mntwana: My dad has no patience whatsoever

12/23/11 2:36:03: UNkosiyazi: who ever said that was misleading you.
12/23/11 2:39:22: Mntwana: If u say so..

12/23/11 2:45:28: UNkosiyazi: enjoy and drive safe.
12/23/11 2:46:21: Mntwana: Thats lovely..
12/23/11 2:47:49: UNkosiyazi: ngiyabonga

12/23/11 2:57:59: UNkosiyazi: AS I LAY ME DOWN TO SLEEP, WORDS FROM
YASIIN BEY (AN ARTIST FORMERLY KNOWN AS MOS DEF) RINGS IN MY EARS
WHEN HE SAYS:
12/23/11 8:13:08: Mntwana: Extracting knowledge from my only
remaining grandfather kwaMntwana

12/23/11 9:12:05: UNkosiyazi: good for you. write it down or video
record it.
12/23/11 9:12:37: Mntwana: Recorded and wrote..

12/23/11 9:13:57: UNkosiyazi: im impressed... indeed, you are a fast
learner.
12/23/11 9:14:28: UNkosiyazi: ps:

12/23/11 9:21:04: UNkosiyazi: you must enlighten me too from what
you've learned. im a sucker for knowledge.
12/23/11 9:21:28: UNkosiyazi: anyway, i had a gud sleep.

12/23/11 9:24:08: Mntwana: Thats news to me, i reserve all comments
and suppress all questions

12/23/11 9:24:17: Mntwana: Glad u slept well

12/23/11 9:25:16: Mntwana: il tell u about it, everything though is
about my family and family line..

12/23/11 9:29:56: UNkosiyazi: if it is personal, keep it personal.
angizithandi izindaba zabantu. ask about COMMON ANCESTOR.
12/23/11 9:33:43: Mntwana: Just need to get data..
12/23/11 9:34:35: Mntwana: Just asked him and he said akusizo
ezakwaMntwana ezinoCOMMON ANCESTOR

12/23/11 9:36:20: Mntwana: uCOMMON ANCESTOR is from my great grandmother's side..and thats all i know right now

12/23/11 9:38:51: UNkosiyazi: cool... how does he feel about Foreign religion(s)?
12/23/11 9:40:18: UNkosiyazi: did you know that everytime you recite or recall izithakazelo zakini you are "praying" to the ancestors?
12/23/11 9:41:50: UNkosiyazi: you can not and you will not escape the religion of our forefathers.
12/23/11 9:44:17: Mntwana: I know I know!!! I know that that was praying to my ancestors.
12/23/11 9:57:34: UNkosiyazi: go get them you Seeker of Truth!

12/23/11 10:00:54: Mntwana: Lol!

12/23/11 10:11:54: UNkosiyazi: <media omitted>

12/23/11 10:12:12: UNkosiyazi: make time to read this...

12/23/11 10:16:37: UNkosiyazi: make time to read this. his company owns LVMH (Louis Vutton, Hennessy, Moet), Cartier, Alfred Dunhill, etc...
12/23/11 12:30:56: Mntwana: <media omitted>

12/23/11 17:42:57: UNkosiyazi: grandpa?

12/23/11 23:56:50: Mntwana: Yea, proof-reading some of my notes

12/23/11 23:59:53: UNkosiyazi: wonderful

12/24/11 0:32:21: Mntwana: Yini impangela?

12/24/11 0:41:30: UNkosiyazi: guinea fowl

12/24/11 0:42:41: Mntwana: Ok.....thanks..

12/24/11 0:43:34: UNkosiyazi: you're welcome.

12/24/11 1:02:02: UNkosiyazi: <media omitted>

12/24/11 1:06:31: Mntwana: Lol, yaz' kodwa
12/24/11 1:07:32: UNkosiyazi: hahaha...

12/24/11 1:33:14: UNkosiyazi: Kanye West: "...50 told me go 'head
switch the style up
12/24/11 1:35:04: UNkosiyazi: Rick Ross: ambition is priceless, it's
in my vein.

12/24/11 1:44:45: Mntwana: Shweet.

12/24/11 1:53:03: UNkosiyazi: you need ambition in life.

12/24/11 1:57:35: Mntwana: Sure. Totaly agree.

12/24/11 1:58:30: Mntwana: Lupe Fiasco
12/24/11 2:04:00: UNkosiyazi: a very conscious rapper. thanks to the
Nation of Islam for instilling structure and values on his parents.

12/24/11 2:09:34: Mntwana: I didn't even know about him until now..i
listen to very little hip-hop

12/24/11 2:12:20: UNkosiyazi: hahaha... stay open-minded. there is
more to life than what meets the eye.

12/24/11 2:15:07: Mntwana: True. I dont argue.

12/24/11 4:09:32: Mntwana: <media omitted>

12/24/11 7:21:35: UNkosiyazi: for a second while downloading i
thought you have gone chiskop.

12/24/11 7:56:47: Mntwana: Lol, i thought that may be the impression that u wud get...but no, il go bald once iv captured a husband lol

12/24/11 7:59:29: Mntwana: Ngisaba kabi ukugunda..

12/24/11 8:00:22: Mntwana: Im afraid it wudnt suit me

12/24/11 9:59:12: UNkosiyazi: hahaha...

12/24/11 10:32:39: UNkosiyazi: try it for one year and see.

12/24/11 10:50:37: UNkosiyazi: you like my smoothie?

12/24/11 10:50:52: UNkosiyazi: <media omitted>

12/24/11 11:31:55: Mntwana: Im using up airtime and data like it's going outa fashion, so i cnt download ur smoothie pic just yet.

12/24/11 11:32:10: Mntwana: Wat did u make it from?

12/24/11 11:34:41: UNkosiyazi: my younger brother made it.

12/24/11 11:40:06: Mntwana: Oh kul..u just gave me ideas.

12/24/11 12:26:03: UNkosiyazi: what ideas?

12/24/11 12:27:12: Mntwana: Wana try sumthn along the lines of a smoothie

12/24/11 12:27:37: Mntwana: Lol, My parents left my brother and I at a petrol station and drove off coz they thought that we were in the car

12/24/11 12:28:15: UNkosiyazi: say it aint so!

12/24/11 12:31:34: Mntwana: Lol, im serious..and i had no fone.

12/24/11 12:34:34: UNkosiyazi: interesting.

12/24/11 12:35:14: UNkosiyazi: <media omitted>

12/24/11 12:35:16: UNkosiyazi: anyway, what are you reading these days?

12/24/11 12:35:59: Mntwana: Nothing actually

12/24/11 12:36:34: UNkosiyazi: im disappointed in you. why?

12/24/11 12:39:57: Mntwana: Coz 4rm morning to evening i've been busy and sleeping sengidiniwe.
12/24/11 12:47:24: UNkosiyazi: say it aint so, cant you "make time" to read a page a day before you sleep or something?

12/24/11 12:49:19: Mntwana: Been trying to everyday..
12/24/11 12:49:47: UNkosiyazi: thank you.

12/24/11 12:50:51: UNkosiyazi: if im not reading im writing. if im not doing both, i am thinking of ideas.

12/24/11 13:02:29: Mntwana: Yea well, thats gud 4u..

12/24/11 13:04:36: UNkosiyazi: it can be good for you too.

12/24/11 13:36:47: Mntwana: Yes it can, as soon as kuncipha ama-responsibilities..

12/24/11 13:37:22: UNkosiyazi: well, alright!

12/24/11 14:19:38: Mntwana: My great-great grandfather's name was uScathulo:)

12/24/11 14:22:09: UNkosiyazi: nice

12/24/11 14:23:31: Mntwana: I think Its the cutest ever, lol

12/24/11 14:24:53: UNkosiyazi: hahaha...
12/24/11 14:29:52: Mntwana: Dad's side

12/24/11 14:30:08: Mntwana: NoPhumetsheni..lol

12/24/11 14:35:54: UNkosiyazi: beautiful names, not these European
names with no meaning or blessing in them.

12/24/11 14:38:13: Mntwana: I gots ta agree wit that statement

12/24/11 14:42:14: UNkosiyazi: it's the truth aint it!

12/24/11 14:43:42: UNkosiyazi: crazyness at the malls today, last
minute shopping for "gifts", no parking.

12/24/11 14:46:20: Mntwana: Totaly is. Id like my kids to only have
zulu names.
12/24/11 14:52:22: UNkosiyazi: we shall never repeat mistakes of our
parents, grandparents or great grandparents.

12/24/11 15:00:54: Mntwana: Absolutely.